DAVID LODGE

# The Man Who Wouldn't Get Up and Other Stories

WITH A FOREWORD AND AFTERWORD BY
THE AUTHOR

**VINTAGE**

1 3 5 7 9 10 8 6 4 2

Vintage
20 Vauxhall Bridge Road,
London SW1V 2SA

Vintage is part of the Penguin Random House group of companies
whose addresses can be found at global.penguinrandomhouse.com

Penguin
Random House
UK

First published by Vintage in 2016

'My Last Missis' appeared in *Areté* in 2015
'A Wedding to Remember' first released by
*Good Housekeeping* in 2013

First published, in a different form, by The Bridgewater Press in 1998

penguin.co.uk/vintage

A CIP catalogue record for this book is available
from the British Library

ISBN 9781784704681

Typeset in India by Thomson Digital Pvt Ltd, Noida, Delhi

Printed and bound in Great Britain by Clays Ltd, St Ives plc

Penguin Random House is committed to a sustainable future
for our business, our readers and our planet. This book is made
from Forest Stewardship Council® certified paper.

# Contents

# Foreword

For a fairly short book, this one has a long and complicated – but I hope interesting – history. In the 1990s my novels were published in German translations by the Zurich-based publishing house Haffmans Verlag. The proprietor, Gerd Haffman, an ebullient, enthusiastic publisher, asked me if I had written any short stories which he could publish as a collection. I looked through my files and told him that there were only six which I thought worthy of being re-printed, obviously insufficient to fill a book. But Haffmans produced many books in attractive small formats, and in 1995 Gerd published my half-dozen tales as *Sommergeschichten – Wintermärchen* (Summer Stories – Winter's Tales), a title I suggested because of their seasonal settings. Some other European publishers of my fiction then asked if they could do the same, and in due course translations in similar formats appeared in Poland, Portugal, Italy and France. But both Bompiani in Italy and Rivages in France preferred to use the title of the first and earliest story for the book. I realised that *The Man Who Wouldn't Get Up and Other Stories* was a more intriguing name for it.

An obvious difference between the novel and the short story is that the reader usually begins a story intending to finish it at a single sitting, whereas one reads a novel in a much more leisurely and irregular fashion, picking it up and putting it down as opportunity or inclination dictate. In a sense, we are always eager to get to the end of a short story, but we may well be sorry to reach the end of a much-loved novel. Whereas the meaning of a novel has something of the openness and multiplicity of life itself, the short story usually has a single 'point' to make, fully revealed to us at its ending, which may take the form of a twist in the plot, the solution of a mystery, or a moment of recognition and enhanced awareness – what James Joyce called, borrowing the language of religion, an 'epiphany'.

Most novelists cut their authorial teeth on the short story, for obvious practical reasons, and I was no exception; but I also managed to complete an entire novel at the age of eighteen. It was unpublishable, but it indicated a bias in favour of the long narrative. When Gerd Haffman published my six stories I vaguely hoped that eventually I might write enough new ones to make up a viable collection for the English language market, but the ideas I got for fiction always seemed to invite the expansive development of the novel form. So when a few years later I received an offer to publish the six stories in English in a limited edition of a hundred copies, I was glad to accept. It meant I would have a few 'Author's copies' to keep as a permanent record of the stories without jeopardising the possibility of publishing them as part of a larger collection in the future. This proposal came from Tom Rosenthal, who had changed my fortunes as a novelist when, as Managing Director of Secker & Warburg, he published *Changing Places* very successfully in 1975, after three other publishers had turned it down. Tom retired from full-time commercial publishing in 1998, but started a small private enterprise at about the same time called the Bridgewater Press, which produced covetable limited editions of books for collectors. His handsome edition of *The Man Who Wouldn't Get Up and Other Stories*, printed on Archival Parchment paper and bound in Ratchford Atlantic cloth or (for an extra premium) quarter Library Calf, was published in 1998.

Cut to the 5th of June 2015, when I received an email letter forwarded by Catherine Cho, assistant to my agent, Jonny Geller, at Curtis Brown.

> **From:** philippine hamen
> **Sent:** 28 May 2015 23:57
> **To:** Geller Office
> **Subject:** Hommage to Mr Lodge
>
> Dear Mr Geller,
>     I have a special request here concerning David Lodge.
>     It is a surprise for him so please can we keep it as such?

I am a fervent lector of David Lodge, and I am a furniture designer-maker; actually this vocation appeared to me after I read the short story 'The Man Who Wouldn't Get Up', which gave me the vision of a special, hybrid piece of furniture that would allow the narrator to virtually stay in bed while being able to still work from the structure I came up with, at equi-distance between a desk and a lounger.

Because this 'vision' decided that I would study furniture, and because it is to me one of the most brilliant short stories ever written, I would like to send a finished piece to the address of the author, as a hommage, as a thank you, and as a solution for 'the man who wouldn't get up'! It might be a metaphorical tale, but the result of it is a very serious and ergonomically studied piece of furniture, which had quite a lot of success at the Salone di Mobile 2015, Milan.

Do you think he would be pleased?

I would need his address.

I could show you pictures of it and videos if it helps.

Thank you for your cooperation!

Kindly, Philippine Hamen

(I am from France and I study furniture in London, after graduating from Modern Literature in La Sorbonne in 2007).

Attached to this message were some very striking photos of the lounger-desk displayed at the Milan exhibition. In a follow-up letter Philippine said that it could be dismantled and packed into a box of manageable size, but Catherine told her that the agency could not collude in sending me a large piece of furniture as a surprise present. She asked me what I wanted to do about this unusual offer. After giving the matter considerable thought I replied to Philippine as follows:

Dear Philippine Hamen,

My literary agent Jonny Geller's assistant, Catherine Cho, has sent to me your letter of 28th May, with its extraordinarily generous offer to present me with the beautiful piece of furniture you have constructed, inspired by my short story 'The Man Who Wouldn't Get Up'. I think it must be the most original tribute ever paid by a reader to an author. I would, of course, love to see it, and try lying on it. The problem is that there is no room in my house in which it could be placed without displacing a more essential piece of furniture.

It seems to me that as well as being a piece of furniture your bed-desk is a 3D work of art, and I am not surprised that it caught people's eyes at the Salone di Mobile. I have been wondering whether I could persuade an art gallery in Birmingham, where I live and am known, to accept the piece as a gift, to exhibit it (perhaps occasionally) and store it safely when it is not on display. Perhaps it could be an installation which viewers could actually lie on, and read through the hole an explanation of why you made the object. From the photos you sent it looks as if you provided some explanatory material in this way when it was displayed in Milan.

I am by no means confident of success in this project, but I am willing to try if you approve. Possibly viewers could listen through headphones to a recording of me reading the short story 'The Man Who Wouldn't Get Up'. Unfortunately the story is not available in print in England. The collection of six stories in which you must have read it, *L'Homme qui ne voulait plus se lever* (Rivages) was not published in the UK except in a small limited edition for collectors, though it has been published in several other foreign countries.

With best wishes, David Lodge

Philippine's response was positive and enthusiastic:

I was honoured, and actually very happy, to read your email. As a child I was used to see your books on the bedside tables of my parents, as a teenager I started to read you and I still am! 'L'Homme qui ne voulait plus se lever' is my favourite short story, and I was very surprised, when I tried to find the English version for the needs of my course, that I was unable to find it anywhere! Anyway, I wanted to thank you because it had a great influence on me and it generated the main furniture project of my academic year!

I think your idea of storing the piece and exhibiting it in a gallery in Birmingham is great, and being able to listen to your voice reading the story would add a fourth dimension to it. I don't know any furniture design project which collaborates that actively with literature and I am very excited about it.

I am aware it is not completely in your hands and that it might not succeed but I am very grateful that you are willing to try.

Best wishes from London, Philippine

Thus encouraged, I pursued my idea. The Birmingham gallery I particularly had in mind was the Ikon, a subsidised gallery exhibiting the work of contemporary artists from Britain and all round the world. It occupies a beautifully restored and converted redbrick Victorian school in Brindley Place, part of Birmingham's central arts and entertainment district, and in addition to its large display rooms the Ikon has a cylindrical tower room where small installations are often shown concurrently with one of the gallery's main exhibitions. This room, which can accommodate half a dozen or so people at a time, seemed to me the ideal place to exhibit Philippine's piece. My wife Mary and I are patrons of the gallery and know the Director, Jonathan Watkins well.

I thought he would be receptive to my idea, and I was right. He embraced it immediately and his colleagues were equally enthusiastic. I went down to London to meet Philippine at the Cass Faculty of Art and Design, a part of London Metropolitan University situated in Whitechapel, where I recognised her as the same tall, slim young woman in jeans who had demonstrated the use of the lounger-desk in the Milan exhibition photos. In person she quickly impressed me as charming, intelligent and perceptive. I was able to see the lounger-desk, which was being prepared for the college's summer show, and admired still more its flowing lines, and its combination of different textures and colours – natural wood, dark grey fabric and steel. I lay prone on it, verifying that it was possible to comfortably read an open book placed on the lower level through the aperture in the top level.

In September Philippine came up to Birmingham to be shown round the Ikon, meet the staff, and have a working lunch with Jonathan and me. He proposed that her creation, eventually entitled *For the Man Who Wouldn't Get Up*, should be exhibited in autumn 2016, to coincide with the Birmingham Literary Festival, so that both institutions could benefit from the associated publicity. Although this meant a long delay, it would give Philippine plenty of time to construct a second, more robust version of the lounger-desk. It also gave me time to consider and extend my own input to this mixed-media event.

My pleasure in the project had from the beginning been qualified by a regret that the story which had inspired

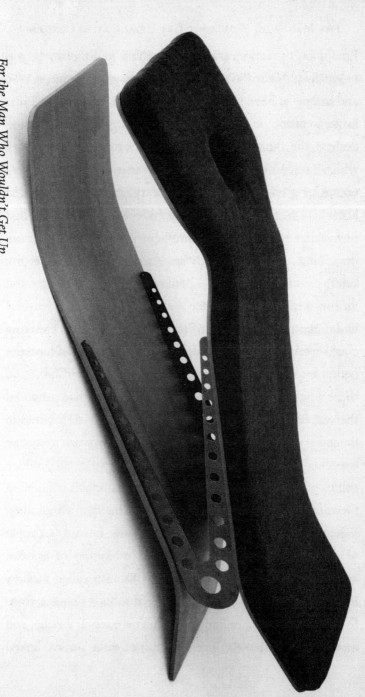

Philippine's creation was not available in English. It was originally published in the *Weekend Telegraph* magazine in 1966 and had never been reprinted except in the Bridgewater Press limited edition of the six stories, so viewers of the lounger-desk at the Ikon whose interest was aroused in the story which it referenced would not be able to satisfy their curiosity except by going to the British Library or another copyright library. It was agreed that Philippine would write the text of a leaflet which would be available at the Ikon exhibition, describing the genesis of the lounger-desk and quoting briefly from the story, but I hankered after giving interested visitors a fuller acquaintance with the text. For that reason I had suggested a recording of myself reading it which visitors could listen to through headphones, but few would have the patience to listen for the twenty minutes it would take, and there would be other practical difficulties. Jonathan proposed that stapled photocopies of the story be freely distributed in the gallery, but I was not disposed to give my work away like a teacher's handout. I wondered if perhaps we could produce copies of a decently printed and bound pamphlet containing the story, which could be purchased from the Ikon's bookshop. When I mentioned this idea to Jonny Geller, he said, 'A couple of years ago the V&A mounted an exhibition of various artists' responses to a story by Hari Kunzru called *Memory Palace*, and they sold a lot of copies of a book about it from their bookshop and online. Why don't we see if Vintage will reprint the Bridgewater Press edition of your stories, linked to the exhibition at the Ikon?' I jumped at this proposal, and immediately saw an opportunity, if it succeeded, to include two new stories I had written recently.

And so it came to pass. The Vintage editorial team liked the old and new stories, none of which they had seen before, and were attracted by the idea of launching the book from an art exhibition. You hold the product of this unlikely sequence of events in your hands. With the addition of the two new stories these eight cover almost the entire span of my life as a published writer of fiction. The first one was written in 1966, the second one at some time in the '70s, the next three belong to the 1980s, 'Pastoral' was written in the early '90s, and the last two very recently. Some are retrospective in their narrative point of view, reflecting changes in manners and morals in society, and they have been placed in yet another time frame with the passing of the years. Tom Rosenthal asked me to write a short introduction to the Bridgewater Press edition describing how and why I came to write the stories, and I have revised and extended these notes in an Afterword to this edition. Philippine Hamen has added a short account of the creative design process that produced her own unique artefact.

D.L., 2016

# The Man Who
# Wouldn't Get Up

His wife was always the first to get up. As soon as the alarm rang she threw back the bedclothes, swung her legs to the floor and pulled on her dressing gown. Her self-discipline filled him with guilt and admiration.

'Now don't go lying in bed,' she said. 'I'm fed up with having your breakfast spoil.' He made no reply, feigning sleep. As soon as she had left the room he rolled over into the warm trough that her body had left in the mattress, and stretched luxuriously. It was the most sensually satisfying moment of his day, this stretch into a new, but warm part of the bed. But it was instantly impaired by the consciousness that he would soon have to get up and face the rest of the day.

He opened one eye. It was still dark, but the street-lamps cast a faint blue illumination into the room. He tested the atmosphere with his breath, and saw it turn to steam. Where one of the curtains was pulled back he could see that ice had formed on the inside of the window. In the course of the morning the ice would melt and the water would roll down to rot the paintwork on the window frame. Some of the water would trickle under the window frame where it would freeze again, jamming the window and warping the wood.

He closed his eye to shut out the painful vision of his house corroding and disintegrating around him. He couldn't, of course, suppress his knowledge of what was wrong with it – of what was wrong, for instance, with the room he lay in: the long jagged crack in the ceiling that ran like a sneer from the electric light fixture to the door, the tear in the lino near the chest of drawers, the cupboard door that hung open because the catch had gone, the wallpaper that bulged in patches where the damp had detached it from the wall, so that it seemed to breathe gently in and out with the opening and shutting of the door . . . He could not suppress his knowledge of all this, but while he was snug under the blankets, with his eyes shut tight, it was all somehow less oppressive, as if it had nothing to do with him personally.

It was only when he left the protection of the warm bed that he would stagger under the combined weight of dissatisfaction with his environment and despair of ever significantly improving it. And, of course, it wasn't just the bedroom. As he passed through the house the evidence of decay and disrepair would greet him at every turn: the dribbling tap in the bathroom, the broken banister on the staircase, the cracked window in the hall, the threadbare patch in the dining-room carpet that would be just a tiny bit bigger than yesterday. And it would be so cold, so cold. Icy draughts needling through keyholes, rattling the letter box, stirring the curtains.

And yet here, in bed, it was so warm and comfortable. The most luxuriously furnished, gas-fired centrally heated, double-glazed and insulated ideal home could not make him more warm and comfortable than he was at this moment.

His wife rattled the poker in the dining-room grate: the dull, metallic sounds were borne to every corner of the house through the water-pipes. It was the signal that breakfast was laid. From the room opposite his own Paul and Margaret, his two children, who had been playing in the cold and the gloom with the cheerful imperviousness to discomfort of the very young, issued boisterously on to the landing and thumped heavily down the stairs. The broken banister creaked menacingly. The dining-room door opened and slammed shut. From the kitchen he heard the distant clamour of cutlery and cooking utensils. He pulled the bedclothes more tightly round his head, muffling his ears and leaving only his nose and mouth free to breathe. He did not want to hear these sounds, harsh reminders of a harsh world.

When he looked beyond the immediate problem of getting up, of coping with the tiresome chores of washing, shaving, clothing and feeding his body, he saw no more inviting prospect before him: only the long walk to the bus stop through streets of houses exactly like his own, the long wait in line, the slow, juddering progress through the choked city streets, and eight hours' drudgery in a poky office which was, like his home, all full of broken things, discoloured, faded, chipped, scratched, grimy, malfunctioning things. Things which said as plainly as the interior of his house: this is your lot; try as hard as you like, but you will never significantly improve it; count yourself lucky if you can prevent it from deteriorating more rapidly.

He tried to gird his spirits preparatory to getting up by reminding himself how fortunate he was compared to many others. He forced his mind to dwell upon the sick and the dying, those in need, those in mental anguish. But the spectacle of human misery thus conjured up merely confirmed his helpless apathy. That others were able to bear these burdens with cheerful resignation gave him no encouragement: what hope had he of emulating them if his present discontents were enough to deprive his life of joy? What comfort was it that his present dreary existence was a fragile crust over an infinitely worse abyss into which he might plunge at any moment? The fact was, he no longer had any love of life. The thought pierced him with a kind of thrill of despair. I no longer love life. There is nothing in life which gives me pleasure any more. Except this: lying in bed. And the pleasure of this is spoiled because I know that I have got to get up. Well, then, why don't I just not get up? Because you've got to get up. You have a job. You have a family to support. Your wife has got up. Your children have got up. They have done their duty. Now you have to do yours. Yes, but it's easy for them. They still love life. I don't any more. I only love this: lying in bed.

He heard, through the wadding of bedclothes, the voice of his wife calling.

'George.' She called flatly, expressionlessly, ritualistically, not expecting an answer. He gave none, but turned over on to his other side, and stretched out his legs. His toes encountered an icy hot-water bottle at the foot of the bed and recoiled. He curled himself up into a foetal posture and withdrew his head completely under the bedclothes. It was warm and dark under the bedclothes, a warm dark cave. He inhaled the warm, fusty air with pleasure, and when it became dangerously deoxygenated he created cunning air-ducts in the bedclothes which admitted fresh air without light.

He heard very faintly his wife calling 'George'. More sharply, imperatively this time. It meant that his family had already consumed their corn-flakes and the bacon was cooked. Now the tension began to build between the longing to stay in bed and the urgency of rising. He contracted his limbs into a tighter coil and wriggled deeper into the mattress as he waited for the third summons.

'George!'

This meant he was now too late for breakfast – might with luck manage to swallow a cup of tea before he rushed out to catch his bus.

For what seemed like a long time, he held his breath. Then he suddenly relaxed and stretched out his limbs. He had decided. He would not get up. The secret was not to think of the consequences. Just to concentrate on the fact of staying in bed. The pleasure of it. The warmth, the comfort. He had free will. He would exercise it. He would stay in bed.

He must have dozed for a while. He was suddenly conscious of his wife in the room.

'It's a quarter past eight. Your breakfast's spoiled . . . George . . . are you getting up? . . . George?' He detected a note of fear in her voice. Suddenly the bedclothes were lifted from his face. He pulled them back, annoyed that all his cunning air-vents had been disturbed.

'George, are you ill?' He was tempted to say, yes, I'm ill. Then his wife would tip-toe away, and tell the children to be quiet, their father was ill. And later she would light a fire in the bedroom and bring him a tray of tempting food. But that was the cowardly course; and the deception would only earn him, at the most, a day's respite from the life he hated. He was nourishing a grander, more heroic plan.

'No, I'm not ill,' he said through the bedclothes.

'Well, get up then, you'll be late for work.' He did not answer, and his wife left the room. He heard her banging about irritably in the bathroom, calling to the children to come and be washed. The lavatory cistern flushed and refilled noisily, the pipes whined and hummed, the children laughed and cried. Outside in the street footsteps hurried past on the pavement, cars wheezed, reluctant to start in the cold morning air, fired and moved away. He lay quiet under the bedclothes, concentrating, contemplating. Gradually he was able to eliminate all these noises from his consciousness. The way he had chosen was a mystical way.

★ ★ ★

The first day was the most difficult. His wife thought he was being merely idle and delinquent, and tried to make him get up by refusing to bring him any food. The fast caused him no great distress, however, and he stuck to his bed all day except for discreet, unobserved visits to the bathroom. When his wife retired that night she was angry and resentful. She complained because she hadn't been able to make the bed properly, and she held herself cold and rigid at the very edge of the mattress furthest from himself. But she was puzzled and guilty too, because he hadn't eaten. There was a note of pleading in her voice when she hoped he would have had enough of this silly nonsense by the next morning.

The next morning was much easier. He simply went off to sleep again as soon as the alarm had stopped ringing, untroubled by guilt or anxiety. It was blissful. Just to turn over and go to sleep again, knowing you weren't going to get up. Later, his wife brought him a breakfast tray and left it, wordlessly, on the floor beside his bed. His children came to the door of the bedroom and stared in at him while he ate. He smiled reassuringly at them.

In the afternoon, the doctor came, summoned by his wife. He marched breezily into the room and demanded, 'Well, now, what appears to be the trouble, Mr Barker?' 'No trouble, Doctor,' he replied gently.

The doctor gave him a brief examination and concluded: 'No reason at all why you shouldn't get out of bed, Mr Barker.' 'I know there isn't,' he replied. 'But I don't want to.'

The next day it was the vicar. The vicar begged him to think of his responsibilities as a husband and father. There were times, one knew only too well, when the struggle to keep going seemed too much to bear, when the temptation simply to give in became almost irresistible . . . But that was not the true Christian spirit. 'Say not the struggle naught availeth . . .'

'What about contemplative monks?' he asked. 'What about hermits, solitaries, column-squatters?'

Ah, but that kind of religious witness, though possibly efficacious in its own time, was not in harmony with modern spirituality. Besides, he could hardly claim that there was anything ascetic or penitential about his particular form of retreat from the world.

'It isn't all roses, you know,' he told the vicar.

And it wasn't. After seven days, he began to get bedsores. After a fortnight, he was too weak to walk unaided to the bathroom. After four weeks he remained permanently confined to his bed, and a nurse was employed to care for his bodily needs. He wasn't sure where the money was coming from to pay for the nurse, or indeed to maintain the house and his family. But he found that simply by not worrying about such problems, they solved themselves.

His wife had lost most of her resentment by now. Indeed he rather thought she respected him more than ever before. He was, he gathered, becoming something of a local, and even national, celebrity. One day a television camera was wheeled into his bedroom, and propped up on the pillows, holding the hand of his wife, he told his story to the viewing millions: how one cold morning he had suddenly realized that he no longer had any love of life, and his only pleasure was in lying in bed, and how he had taken the logical step of lying in bed for the rest of his life, which he did not expect to be protracted much longer, but every minute of which he was enjoying to the full.

After the television broadcast, the trickle of mail through the letter box became a deluge. His eyes were growing weak, and he relied on volunteers from the parish to help him with the correspondence.

Most of the letters pleaded with him to give life another chance, enclosing money or offers of lucrative employment. He declined the offers politely, and banked the money in his wife's name. (She used some of it to have the house redecorated; it amused him to watch the painters clambering about the bedroom; when they whitewashed the ceiling he covered his head with a newspaper.) There was a smaller, but to him more significant number of letters sending him encouragement and congratulations. 'Good luck to you, mate', said one of them, 'I'd do the same if I had the guts.' And another, written on the notepaper of a famous university, said: 'I deeply admire your witness to the intolerable quality of modern life and to the individual's inalienable right to opt out of it: you are an existentialist saint.' Though he wasn't clear about the meaning of all these words, they pleased him. Indeed, he had never felt so happy and so fulfilled as he did now.

And now, more than ever, he thought it would be sweet to die. Though his body was washed and fed and cared for, he felt vitality slowly ebbing away from it. He longed to put on immortality. It seemed as if he had solved not only the problem of life, but the problem of death too. There were times when the ceiling above his head became the canvas for some vision such as the old painters used to draw on the roofs of chapels: he seemed to see angels and saints peering down at him from a cloudy empyrean, beckoning him to join them. His body felt strangely weightless, as if only the bedclothes restrained it from rising into the air. Levitation! or even . . . apotheosis! He fumbled with the blankets and sheets, but his limbs were weak. Then, with a supreme effort, he wrenched the bedclothes aside and flung them to the floor.

He waited, but nothing happened. He grew cold. He tried to drag the blankets back on to the bed, but the effort of throwing them off had exhausted him. He shivered. Outside it was getting dark. 'Nurse,' he called faintly; but there was no response. He called his wife, 'Margaret', but the house remained silent. His breath turned to steam on the cold air. He looked up at the ceiling, but there were no heads of angels and saints looking down:

only a crack in the plaster that ran like a sneer from the door to the light fixture. And suddenly he realised what his eternity was to be. 'Margaret! Nurse!' he cried hoarsely. 'I want to get up! Help me up!'

But no one came.

# The Miser

After the War there was a terrible shortage of fireworks. During the War there hadn't been any fireworks at all; but that was because of the blackout, and because the fireworks-makers were making bombs instead. When the War ended everybody said all the pre-war things, like fireworks, would come back. But they hadn't.

Timothy's mother said the rationing was disgraceful, and his father said they wouldn't catch him voting Labour again, but fireworks weren't even rationed. Rationing would have been fair, anyway, even if it was only six each, or say twelve. Twelve different ones. But there just weren't any fireworks to be had, unless you were very lucky. Sometimes boys at school brought them in, and let off the odd banger in the bogs, for a laugh. They spoke vaguely of getting them 'down the Docks', or from a friend of their dad's, or from a shop that had discovered some pre-war stock, and sold out the same day.

Timothy and Drakey and Woppy had searched all over the neighbourhood for such a shop. Once they did find a place advertising fireworks, but when the man brought them out they were all the same kind, bangers. You couldn't have a proper Guy Fawkes Night with just bangers. Besides, they weren't one of the proper makes, like Wells, Standard or Payne's. They were called 'Whizzo', and had a suspiciously home-made look about them. They cost tenpence each, which was a shocking price to charge for bangers. In the end they bought two each and, with only three weeks to go before November the Fifth, that was still their total stock.

One day Timothy's mother set his heart leaping when she came in from shopping and announced that she had got some fireworks for him. But when she produced them they were only the sparkler things that you held in your hand – little kids' stuff. He'd been so sulky that in the end his mother wouldn't let him have the sparklers, which he rather regretted afterwards.

None of them, not even Drakey, who was the oldest, had a clear memory of Guy Fawkes Night before the War. But they all remembered VJ Night, when there was a bonfire on the bomb-site in the middle of the street where the flying-bomb had fallen, and the sky was gaudy with rockets, and a man from one of the houses at the end of the street had produced two whole boxes of super fireworks, saying he'd saved them for six years for this night. The next morning Timothy had roamed the bomb-site and collected all the charred cases as, in previous years, he had collected shrapnel. That was when he had first learned the haunting names – 'Chrysanthemum Fire', 'Roman Candle', 'Volcano', 'Silver Rain', 'Torpedo', 'Moonraker' – beside which the 'Whizzo Banger' struck a false and unconvincing note.

One Saturday afternoon Timothy, Drakey and Woppy wandered far from their home ground, searching for fireworks. The best kind of shop was the kind that sold newspapers, sweets, tobacco and a few toys. They found several new ones, but had no luck. Some of the shops even had notices in the window: 'No Fireworks'.

'If they had any,' said Drakey bitterly, 'I bet they wouldn't sell them. They'd keep them for their own kids.'

'Let's go home,' said Woppy. 'I'm tired.'

On the way home they played 'The Lost Platoon', a game based on a serial story in Drakey's weekly comic. Drakey was Sergeant McCabe, the leader of the platoon, Timothy was Corporal Kemp, the quiet, clever one, and Woppy was 'Butch' Baker, the strong but rather stupid private. The platoon was cut off behind enemy lines and the game consisted in avoiding the observation of Germans. Germans were anyone who happened to be passing.

'Armoured vehicles approaching,' said Timothy.

Drakey led them into the driveway of a private golf course. They lay in some long grass while two women with prams passed on the pavement. Timothy glanced idly round him, and sat up sharply.

'Look!' he breathed, scarcely able to believe such luck. About thirty yards away, on some rough ground screened from the road by the golf-club fence, was a ramshackle wooden shed. Leaning against one wall was a notice, crudely painted on a wooden board. 'Fireworks for Sale', it said.

Slowly they got to their feet and, with silent, wondering looks at each other, approached the shed. The door was open, and inside an old man was sitting at a table, reading a newspaper and smoking a pipe. A faded notice over his head said: 'Smoking Prohibited'. He looked up and took the pipe out of his mouth.

'Yes?' he said.

Timothy looked for help to Drakey and Woppy, but they were just gaping at the man and at the dusty boxes piled on the floor.

'Er . . . you haven't any fireworks, have you?' Timothy ventured at last.

'Yes, I've got a few left, son. Want to buy some?'

The fireworks were sold loose, not in pre-packed boxes, which suited them perfectly. They took a long time over their selection, and it was dark by the time they had spent all their money. On the way home they stopped under each lamp-post to open their paper bags and reassure themselves that their treasure was real. The whole episode had been like a dream, or a fairy tale, and Timothy was afraid that at any moment the fireworks would dissolve.

As they reached the corner of their street, Timothy said: 'Whatever you do, don't tell anybody where we got them.'

'Why?' said Woppy.

'So that we can go back and get some more, before he sells out.'

'I've spent all my fireworks money anyway,' said Drakey.

'Yes, but it's ages to Guy Fawkes, and we've got pocket money to come,' argued Timothy.

But when they went back the following Saturday, the shed was locked, and the notice was gone. They peered through the windows, but there was only dusty furniture to be seen.

'Must have sold out,' said Drakey. But there was something creepy about the sudden disappearance of the fireworks man, and they hurried away from the shed and never spoke of it again.

Each evening, as soon as he got home from school, Timothy got out the box in which he had put his fireworks and counted them. He took them all out and arranged them, first according to size, then according to type, then according to price. He pored over the brightly coloured labels, studying intently the blurred instructions: hold in a gloved hand, place in earth and stand well back, nail to a wooden post. He handled the fireworks with great care, grudging every grain of gunpowder that leaked out and diminished the glory to come.

'I wonder you keep those things under your bed,' said his mother. 'Remember what happened to the sweets.'

About a year previously, an American relative had sent Timothy a large box of 'candies', as she called them. Their bright wrappings and queer names – *Oh Henry!*, *Lifesavers* and *Baby Ruth* – had fascinated him much as the fireworks did; and he was so overwhelmed by the sense of his own wealth amid universal sweet-rationing that he had hoarded them under his bed and ate them sparingly. But they had started to go mouldy, and attracted mice, and his mother threw them away.

'Mice don't eat fireworks,' he said to her, stroking the stick of his largest rocket. But on second thoughts, he asked his mother to keep them for him in a warm, dry cupboard.

'How d'you know they'll go off, anyway?' said his father. 'Pre-war, aren't they? Probably dud by now.'

Timothy knew his father was teasing, but he took the warning seriously. 'We'll have to try one,' he said solemnly to Drakey and Woppy. 'To see if they're all right. We'd better draw lots.'

'I don't mind letting off one of mine,' said Drakey.

'No, I want to let off one of mine,' said Woppy.

In the end, they let off one each. Woppy chose a 'Red Flare', and Drakey a 'Roman Candle'. Timothy couldn't understand why they didn't let off the cheapest ones. They went to the bomb-site to let them off. For a few dazzling seconds the piles of rubble, twisted iron, planks and rusty water cisterns were illuminated with garish colour. When it was over they blinked in the dim light of the street-lamps and grinned at each other.

'Well, they work all right,' said Drakey.

The other two tried to persuade Timothy to let off one of his. He was tempted, but he knew he would regret it later, and refused. They quarrelled, and Drakey taunted Timothy with being a Catholic like Guy Fawkes. Timothy said that he didn't care, that you didn't have to be against Guy Fawkes to have fireworks, and that he wasn't interested in the Guy part anyway. He went home alone, got out his fireworks, and sat in his bedroom all the evening, counting and arranging them.

Once Drakey and Woppy had broken into their store, they could not restrain themselves till November the Fifth. They started with one firework a night, then it went up to two, then it was three. Drakey had a talent for discovering new and spectacular ways of using them. He would drop a lighted banger into an old water tank and produce an explosion that brought the neighbours to their doors, or he would shoot a 'Torpedo' out of a length of drain-pipe. Timothy had a few ideas of his own, but, as he stubbornly refused to use any of his own fireworks, the most he could ask was to be a passive spectator. His turn would come on November the Fifth, when the empty-handed Drakey and Woppy would be glad to watch his display.

On the evening of November 4th, Timothy counted his collection for the last time.

'You'll be lost without those things after tomorrow,' said his mother.

'I don't believe he really wants to set them off,' said his father.

''Course I do,' said Timothy. But he closed the lid of the box with a sigh.

'I'll be glad to see the back of them, anyway,' said his mother. 'Now, who could that be?'

His father answered the door. The policeman was so big he seemed to fill the entire room. He smiled encouragingly at Timothy, but Timothy just hugged his box to his chest, and looked at his feet.

'Look, Sergeant,' said his father, 'I realise that if these fireworks are really stolen goods—'

'Not exactly stolen, sir,' said the policeman. 'But as good as. This old codger just broke into the storage shed and set up shop.'

'Well, what I mean is, I know you're entitled to take them away, but this is a special case. You know what kids are like about fireworks. He's been looking forward to Guy Fawkes Night for weeks.'

'I know, sir, I've got kids myself. But I'm sorry. This is the only lot we've been able to trace. We'll need them for evidence.' He turned to Timothy. 'D'you happen to know, sonny, if any of your friends bought fireworks off the same man?'

Timothy nodded speechlessly, trying not to cry. 'But I'm the only one that saved them,' he said; and with the words the tears rolled uncontrollably down his cheeks.

# My First Job

You don't have to be Protestant to have the Protestant ethic, I tell my students, when we come to Weber in my survey course on Sociological Grand Theory. Look at me, I say: Jewish father, Catholic mother – and I develop an allergic rash at the mere mention of the word 'holiday', with all its connotations of reckless expenditure of time and money. Accumulate, accumulate! – that's my motto, whether it's publications, index cards, or those flimsier bits of paper that promise to pay the bearer so many pounds if he presents them to the Bank of England. Work! Strive! Excel! For the job's own sake! My students, lolling in their seats, mentally preoccupied with the problem of how to draw the dole *and* hitch-hike to Greece this summer, grin tolerantly and unbelievingly at me through their beards and fringes. Sometimes, to try and make them understand, I tell them the story of my first job.

Once upon a time, in the olden days, or, to be more precise, in the summer of 1952 (so I begin), at the age of seventeen and three-quarters, I got my first job, selling newspapers and magazines off a little trolley on Waterloo Station. It was a temporary job, to fill in a few weeks between getting my A-level results (which were excellent, I need hardly say) and going to university. There was no real economic need for me to work, and the weekly wage of £3:10s:0d (even allowing for subsequent inflation) made it scarcely worthwhile to travel up daily from my home in Greenwich. It was a matter of principle. My father, who ran his own dressmaking business employing thirty people (which he intended to hand on to me, his only child), was dubious of the point or profit of a university education, and determined that at least I should not loaf idly about the house while I waited to commence it. It was he who spotted the advert in the *Evening Standard*, phoned up the manager of the shop, and talked him into giving me the job on a temporary basis, without even consulting me. My mother looked at the advertisement. 'It says, "suitable school-leaver",' she observed.

'Well, he's left school, hasn't he?' demanded my father.

'"School-leaver" means some no-hope fifteen-year-old from a secondary modern,' said my mother. 'It's a euphemism.' She was a well-educated woman, my mother. 'Pays like a euphemism, too,' she added. Years of marriage to my father had imparted a Jewish edge to her Irish sense of humour.

'Never mind, it will give him an idea of what the real world is like,' said my father. 'Before he buries his head in books for another three years.'

'It's true, he ought to give his eyes a rest,' my mother agreed.

This conversation took place in the kitchen. I overheard it, sitting in the dining room, going through my stamp collection (I was totting up the value of all my stamps in the Stanley Gibbons catalogue: I seemed to be worth thousands, though I had no intention of selling). I was *meant* to overhear the conversation, and to be ready to give an answer when the substance of it was formally put to me. Diplomatic leaks of this kind oiled the wheels of family life wonderfully.

My father came into the dining room. 'Oh, there you are,' he said, affecting surprise. 'I've found a job for you.'

'What kind of job?' I enquired coyly. I had already decided to accept it.

The next Monday morning, I presented myself, promptly at 8.30, at the bookstall, a large green island in the middle of Waterloo Station. Waves of office workers arriving on suburban trains surged across the station precinct as if pursued by demons, pausing only to snatch newspapers and magazines from the counters of the shop for the next stage of their journeys by tube or bus. Inside the shop, in a cramped and stuffy little office, seated at a desk heaped with invoices and ringed with the traces of innumerable mugs of tea, was the manager, Mr Hoskyns: a harassed, irascible little man who had evidently suffered a stroke or some kind of palsy, since the right-hand side of his face was paralysed and the corner of his mouth was held up by a little gold hook and chain suspended from his spectacles. Out of the other corner of his mouth he asked me how much change I would give from a ten-shilling note to a customer who had bought three items costing ninepence, two and sixpence, and a penny-ha'penny, respectively. Suppressing an urge to remind him that I had just passed A-level Maths-with-Stats with flying colours, I patiently answered the question, with a speed that seemed to impress him. Then Mr Hoskyns took me outside to where two youths loitered beside three mobile news-stands. These were green-painted wooden barrows, their steeply angled sides fitted with racks for displaying magazines and newspapers.

'Ray! Mitch! This 'ere's the new boy. Show 'im the ropes,' said Mr Hoskyns, and disappeared back into his lair.

Ray was a boy of about my stature, though (I guessed) about a year younger. He was smoking a cigarette which dangled rakishly from his lower lip, and which he occasionally transferred from one side to the other without using his hands, as if to demonstrate that in one respect at least he had an advantage over Mr Hoskyns. He kept his hands plunged into the pockets of an Army Surplus windbreaker, and wore heavy boots protruding from frayed trousers. Mitch (I never did discover whether this was a nickname or a contraction of a real first or second name) was very small and of indeterminate age. He had a dirty, wizened little face like a monkey's, and bit his nails continuously. He wore a collarless shirt and the jacket and trousers of two different striped suits, of the kind working-class boys often wore for Sunday best in cheap imitation of their fathers; the jacket was brown and the trousers were blue, and both garments were in a state of considerable disrepair. They looked at me in my grey flannels and the grammar school blazer which, on the advice of my mother, I had decided to 'wear out' on the job, since I would have no further use for it.

'Wotcher wanner dead-end job like this for then?' was Ray's first utterance.

'I'm only doing it for a month,' I said. 'Just while I'm waiting to go to university.'

'University? Yer mean, like Oxford and Cambridge? The Boat Race and that?' (It should be remembered that going to university was a rarer phenomenon in 1952 than it is now.)

'No, London University. The London School of Economics.'

'Whaffor?'

'To get a degree.'

'What use is that to yer?'

I pondered a short, simple answer to this question. 'You get a better job in life afterwards,' I said at length. I didn't bother to explain that personally I wouldn't be looking for a job, since a thriving little business was being kept warm for me. Mitch, nibbling at his fingers, stared at me intently, like a savage pigmy surprised by the appearance of a white explorer in the jungle.

Mr Hoskyns popped an angry head round the door. 'I thought I said, "Show 'im the ropes," didn't I?'

The ropes were simple enough. You loaded your trolley with newspapers and magazines, and trundled off to platforms where trains were filling up prior to their departure. There were no kiosks on the actual platforms of Waterloo Station in those days, and we were meant to serve passengers who had passed through the ticket barriers without providing themselves with reading matter. The briskest trade came from the boat trains that connected at Southampton with the transatlantic liners (remember them?), whose passengers always included a quota of Americans anxious to free their pockets of the heavy British change. Next in importance were the expresses to the holiday resorts and county towns of the south-west, especially the all-Pullman *Bournemouth Belle*, with its pink-shaded table lamps at every curtained window. The late-afternoon and early-evening commuting crowds, cramming themselves back into the same grimy carriages that had disgorged them in the morning, bought little except newspapers from us. Our brief was simply to roam the station in search of custom. When our stocks were low, we pushed our trolleys back to the shop to replenish them. Brenda, a pleasant young married woman with elaborately permed hair, who served behind the counter, would give us the items we asked for and make a note of the quantities.

I did not dislike the work. Railway stations are places of considerable sociological interest. The subtle gradations of the British class-system are displayed there with unparalleled richness and range of illustration. You see every human type, and may eavesdrop on some of the most deeply emotional moments in people's lives: separations and reunions of spouses and sweethearts, soldiers off to fight in distant wars, families off to start a new life in the Dominions, honeymoon couples off to . . . whatever honeymoon couples did. I had only very hazy ideas about that, having been too busy swotting for my A-levels to spare much time for thinking about sex, much less having any, even the solitary kind. When Ray told me on my second day that I ought to have some copies of the *Wanker's Times* on my trolley, I innocently went and asked Brenda for some. The word was new to me. As for the activity to which it referred, my father had effectively warned me off that in his Facts of Life talk when I was fourteen. (This talk was also delivered ostensibly to my mother while I eavesdropped in the dining room. 'I never wasted my strength when I was a lad, you know what I mean?' my father loudly declared. 'I saved it for the right time and place.' 'I should think so too,' said my mother.) Brenda turned brick red, and went off muttering to complain to Mr Hoskyns, who came bouncing out of his office, impassive on one side of his face, angry on the other.

'What's the idea, insulting Brenda like that? You'd better wash your mouth out, my lad, or out you go on your arse.' He checked himself, evidently recognising my bewilderment was genuine. 'Did Ray put you up to it, then?' He sniggered, and shook his shoulders in suppressed mirth, making the little golden chain chink faintly. 'All right, I'll speak to 'im. But don't be so simple, another time.' Across the station's expanse, lurking beside the Speak Your Weight machine, I could see Ray and Mitch watching this scene with broad grins on their faces, nudging and jostling each other. 'And by the way,' Mr Hoskyns threw over his shoulder as he returned to his office, 'we never send out *'Ealth and Efficiency* on the trolleys.' (*Health and Efficiency*, I usually have to explain to the children at this point, was one of the very few publications on open sale, in those days, in which one might examine photographs of the naked female form, tastefully disposed among sand dunes, or clasping strategically positioned beach-balls.)

At the end of the day we took our money to be counted by Mr Hoskyns and entered in his ledger. On my first day I took £3:15s:6d, Mitch £5:7s:8d, and Ray £7:0s:1d. It wasn't really surprising that I lagged behind the other two, because they knew from experience the times and locations of the trains that provided the best custom. By the following Friday, the busiest day of the week, I had almost caught up with Mitch – £8:19s:6d to his £9:1s:6d – though Ray had taken £10:15s:9d.

'What's the highest amount you've ever taken in one day?' I asked, as we left the shop, pocketing our meager wages, and preparing to join the homegoing crowds. It irked me somewhat that these secondary modern types, even allowing for their greater experience, were able to take more cash than me. It bothered me much more than the practical joke over *Health and Efficiency*.

'Ray took eleven parn nineteen 'n' six one Friday,' said Mitch. 'That's the all-time record.'

Fatal phrase! Like the smell of liquor to an alcoholic. The job was suddenly transformed into a contest – like school, like examinations, except that one's performance was measured in £sd instead of percentage marks. I set myself to beat Ray's record the following Friday. I still remember the shocked, unbelieving expressions on Ray's and Mitch's faces as Mr Hoskyns called out my total.

'Twelve pounds eggs-*actly*! Well done, lad! That's the best ever, I do believe.'

The following day, Saturday, I noticed that Ray was assiduously working the long lines of holidaymakers queuing for the special trains to the seaside resorts, milking their custom before they ever got to the platforms where Mitch and I plied our trade. When Mr Hoskyns announced the tallies at the end of the day, Ray had taken £12:7s:8d – a new record, and particularly remarkable in being achieved on a Saturday.

Suddenly, we were locked in fierce competition. Economically, it was quite absurd, for we were paid no commission on sales – though Mr Hoskyns certainly was, and manifested understandable pleasure as our daily and weekly takings escalated. At the sound of our trolleys returning in the late afternoon, he would come out of his cubbyhole to greet us with a lopsided smile, his gold chain glinting in the pale sunlight that slanted through the grimy glass of the station roof. The old record of £11:19s:6d soon seemed a negligible sum – something any one of us could achieve effortlessly on a wet Monday or Tuesday. On the third Friday of my employment, we grossed over fifty pounds between us. Ray's face was white and strained as Mr Hoskyns called out the totals, and Mitch gnawed his fingernails like a starving cannibal reduced to self-consumption. Mitch had taken £14:10s:3d, Ray £18:4s:9d and myself £19:1s:3d.

The following week was my last on the job. Aware of this fact, Ray and Mitch competed fiercely to exceed my takings, while I responded eagerly to the challenge. We ran, literally ran, with our trolleys from platform to platform, as one train departed and another began to fill up. We picked out rich-looking Americans in the boat-train crowd and hung about in their vicinity with our most expensive magazines, *Vogue* and *Harper's Bazaar*, that cost a whole half-crown each, prominently displayed. We developed an eye for the kind of young man on the *Bournemouth Belle* who would try to impress his girlfriend with a lavish expenditure of money on magazines that clearly neither of them would be reading. We shuffled our stocks and rearranged them several times a day to appeal to the clientele of the moment. We abbreviated our lunch-hour and took our teabreaks on the move. In takings, Ray and I were neck and neck, day by day: sometimes he was the winner by a few shillings, sometimes myself. But the real needle match between us was on the Friday, which was to be my last day of work, since I had earned some overtime which entitled me to have the last Saturday off. Both Ray and I realised that this Friday would see the record smashed yet again, and perhaps the magic figure of £20 in a single day – the four-minute mile of our world – achieved by one or other of us.

Recklessly we raced across the station with our trolleys that day, to claim the most favourable pitches beside the first-class compartments of departing expresses; jealously we eyed each other's dwindling stocks. Like Arab street-traders we accosted astonished passengers and pestered them to buy our wares, forcing our way into intimate circles of tearfully embracing relatives, or tapping urgently on the windows of carriages whose occupants had already settled themselves for a quiet snooze. At one point I saw Ray actually running beside a moving train to complete the sale of a copy of *Homes and Gardens.*

At the end of the day, Mitch had taken £15:8s:6d, Ray £20:1s:9d and myself £21:2s:6d. Ray turned away, sick and white, and ground the cigarette he had been smoking under his heel. Mitch swore softly and drew blood from his mutilated finger ends. I felt suddenly sorry for them both. The future stretched out for me as rosy as the table lamps of the *Bournemouth Belle.* Within a few years, I had reason to hope, it would be I who would be taking his seat for luncheon on the plump Pullman cushions; and although I didn't actually guess that before many more had passed I would be catching the boat train for the *Queen Mary* and a Fellowship in the United States, I had a hunch that such extended horizons would one day be mine. While for Ray and Mitch the future held only the prospect of pushing the trolleys from platform to platform, until perhaps they graduated to serving behind the counters of the shop – or, more likely, became porters or cleaners. I regretted, now, that I had won the competition for takings, and denied them the small satisfaction of beating me in that respect at least. But the worst was still to come.

Mr Hoskyns was paying me off: three one-pound notes and a ten-shilling note. 'You've done well, son,' he said. 'Sales from the trolleys have turned up a treat since you came 'ere. You've shown these two idle little sods what 'ard work really means. And mark my words,' he continued, turning to Ray and Mitch, 'I expect you two to keep up the good work after 'e's gorn. If you don't turn in this sort of sum every Friday, from now on, I'll want to know the reason why – you understand?'

The next day, I overheard my parents talking in the kitchen. 'He seems very moody,' said my mother. 'Do you think he's fallen in love?' My father snorted derisively. 'In love? He's probably just constipated.' 'He seemed very quiet when he came home from work yesterday,' said my mother. 'You'd almost think he was sorry to leave.' 'He's probably wondering whether it's a good idea to go to university after all,' said my father. 'Well, he can come straight into the business now, if he wants to.'

I burst into the kitchen. 'I'll tell you why I'm moody!' I cried.

'You shouldn't listen to other people's private conversations,' said my mother.

'It's because I've seen how capitalism exploits the workers! How it sets one man against another, cons them into competing with each other, and takes all the profit. I'll have nothing more to do with it!'

My father sank on to a kitchen chair with a groan, and covered his face with his hands. 'I knew it, I knew it would happen one day. My only son, who I have been slaving for all these years, has had a brainstorm. What have I done to deserve that this should happen to me?'

So that was how I became a sociologist. My first job was also my last. (I don't call this a job – reading books and talking about them to a captive audience; I would pay to do it if they weren't paying me.) I didn't, as you see, go into business; I went into academic life, where the Protestant ethic does less harm to one's fellow men. But the faces of Ray and Mitch still haunt me, as I last saw them, with the realisation slowly sinking in that they were committed to maintaining that punishing tempo of work, that extraordinary volume of sales, indefinitely, and to no personal advantage, or else be subjected to constant complaint and abuse. All because of me.

After my lecture on Weber, I usually go back to Marx and Engels.

# Where the Climate's Sultry

Long, long ago, in August 1955, before the Pill or the Permissive Society had been invented, four young people from England struggled inexpertly with their sexual appetites on the island of Ibiza, which, as a place of popular British resort, also had yet to be invented. Ibiza was still an exotic destination in those days, one the departing holiday-maker might let drop without self-deprecation – with, indeed, a certain air of adventurousness. It was certainly an adventure for Desmond, Joanna, Robin and Sally.

Des, Jo, Rob and Sal – thus were they known to each other, the less essential syllables of their names having worn away under continual use – had first met and paired off at a Freshers' Hop in their second week at a redbrick provincial university. Elective affinities drew them together in that milling throng of anxious and excitable youth. Each of them, unnerved by the sexual competitiveness of their new environment, was looking, half-consciously, for an agreeable, presentable companion of the opposite sex who would settle, once and for all, the question of who to 'go around with'. They chose well. Over the next three years, while their contemporaries changed partners with fickle frequency, or remained for ever starved and solitary on the edge of the dance, while all around them jilted boys took to drink, and forsaken girls wept into their tutors' handkerchiefs, while rash engagements were painfully dissolved, and nervous breakdowns spread like flu, the twin relationships of Desmond and Joanna, Robin and Sally, remained serene and stable: a fixed, four-starred constellation in an expanding and fissile universe.

Both girls were doing a general Arts degree, and the boys were doing Chemistry. Outside lectures, they formed an inseparable quartet. In their second year, as University regulations permitted, the girls rented a bed-sitting room, and here all four ate and studied together in the evenings. At ten o'clock they made a final cup of coffee and dimmed the lights. Then for half an hour or so, until it was time for the boys to return to their digs, they reclined on twin divans for a cuddle. Nothing more than a cuddle was possible in the circumstances, but this arrangement suited them well. Joanna and Sally were nice girls, and Desmond and Robin were considerate young men. Both couples vaguely assumed that eventually they would get married, but this possibility seemed at once too remote and too real to be anticipated. If three was a crowd, four was company in this situation. Indeed, while fondling each other on their respective divan beds, the two couples would often maintain a lively four-pointed conversation across the space between them.

All worked hard as Finals approached. They planned to reward themselves, and round off their undergraduate careers, with what Desmond described as 'a slap-up Continental holiday, somewhere off the beaten track', to be financed by a month's work in a frozen-food factory. It was a measure of what sensible, responsible young people they were that not one of the eight parents concerned raised any objection to this plan. They perhaps reckoned without the effect of a Mediterranean atmosphere upon placid English temperaments. As Joanna, who had prepared a question on Byron for her Finals, liked to quote, with almost obsessive frequency, in Ibiza:

> *What men call gallantry, and gods adultery,*
> *Is much more common where the climate's sultry.*

★ ★ ★

There was no airport in Ibiza in those days. A student charter flight in a shuddering old Dakota took them to Barcelona, where they embarked the same evening on a boat bound for the Balearic Islands. Desmond and Robin sat up on deck, where the girls joined them at dawn to watch, with suitable exclamations, the white, steeply raked façade of the town of Ibiza rise slowly out of the turquoise Mediterranean. They breakfasted on rolls and coffee outside a quayside café, feeling the sun already burning between their shoulder-blades. Then they took a bus across the island, where they had booked into a *pensión* at a more sheltered resort with a beach.

At first they were quite content with swimming, sunbathing and the other simple diversions of the little resort: the cafés and *bodegas* where alcohol was so absurdly cheap, the shops selling gaudy basket-work and leather goods, and the rather pretentiously named 'nightclubs' where, for the price of a bottle of sweet Spanish champagne, you could dance on a concrete floor to the jerky rhythm of a three-piece band and occasionally witness an amateurish but spirited performance of flamenco dancing. The young people conducted themselves with their habitual decorum and amiability, and the proprietress of the *pensión*, who had regarded them somewhat suspiciously on their arrival, now beamed at them as they came in for the somewhat repetitive but decent fare she served: soup, fish or veal, chips, salad and water melon.

The loss of innocence began, perhaps, with an awareness of their enhanced physical attractiveness. The pallor of study and factory work was burned away by the southern sun in a matter of days, and they looked at each other as into an artificially tinted ballroom mirror, with little thrills of pleasurable surprise. How handsome, how pretty they were! How becoming was Joanna's freckled tan against her sunbleached hair, how trim and limber Sally's brown limbs in her yellow swimsuit, how fit and virile the boys looked on the beach, or dressed for the evening in white shirts and natty lightweight slacks.

Then the rhythm of the Spanish day was itself an invitation to sensual indulgence. They got up late, breakfasted and went to the beach. At about two they returned to the *pensión* for lunch, with which they drank a good deal of wine. They then retired to their rooms for a siesta. At six, showered and changed, they took a stroll and an aperitif. They dined at eight-thirty, and afterwards went out again, into the silky Mediterranean night, to a favourite *bodega* where, sitting round a bare wooden table, they conscientiously sampled every liqueur known to the Balearic Islands. Sometime after midnight they returned to the *pensión*, a little unsteady on their feet, giggling and shushing each other on the stairs. They all went into the girls' room and Joanna brewed them instant coffee with a little electric gadget that you immersed in a cup of water. Then they cuddled for a while on the twin beds. But the hours they learned to identify as the most erotically exciting were those of the siesta, when they lay on their beds in their underclothes, replete with food and drink, sleepy but seldom asleep, dazed by the heat that pressed against the closed shutters, limp, unresisting vessels of idle thoughts and desires. One afternoon Desmond and Robin were lying on their beds in their Y-fronts, Robin browsing listlessly in an old copy of the *New Statesman* he had brought with him, and Desmond staring, hypnotised, at the closed shutters, where sunlight was seeping through the cracks like molten metal, when there was a knock on the door. It was Sally.

'Are you decent?'

Robin answered: 'No.'

'In the nude?'

'No.'

'That's all right then.'

Sally came into the room. Neither boy moved to cover himself. Somehow it seemed too much of an effort in the heat. In any case, Sally's own knickers were clearly visible beneath the shirt, borrowed from Robin, that she was wearing by way of a negligee.

'What d'you want?' said Robin.

'Company. Jo's asleep. Move up a bit.'

Sally sat down on Robin's bed.

'Ouch, mind my sun-burn,' he said.

Desmond closed his eyes and listened for a while to the whispers, giggles, rustlings and creakings from the other bed. 'In case you haven't noticed,' he said at length, 'I'm trying to have a siesta.'

'Why don't you take my bed, then?' said Sally. 'It's quiet in there.'

'Good idea,' said Desmond, getting up and putting on his bathrobe.

After he had left, Sally snickered.

'What?' said Robin.

'Jo's got nothing on.'

'Really nothing?'

'Not a stitch.'


Desmond knocked on the door of the girls' room. There was no reply, so he put his head round the door. Joanna was asleep, with her back towards him. Her buttocks, white against her tan, shone palely, like twin moons, in the shuttered room. He hastily closed the door and stood still in the corridor, his heart thumping. Then he knocked again, more firmly.

'What? Who is it?'

'It's me – Des.'

'Just a mo. All right.'

He went in. Joanna had covered herself with a sheet. She was flushed and her hair was stuck to her forehead with perspiration. 'Is it time to get up?' she asked.

'No. Rob and Sal are larking about in our room, so I've come to have my siesta in here.'

'Oh.'

'Is that all right?'

'Make yourself at home.'

Desmond lay down on Sally's bed in the attitude of a soldier standing to attention.

'You don't look very relaxed,' said Joanna.

'Can I lie down with you?'

'All right.' He was across the room in a flash. 'As long as you stay outside the sheet,' she added.

'Why?'

'I've got nothing on.'

'Haven't you?'

'It's so hot.'

'It is, isn't it.' Desmond took off his bathrobe.

'*And so they make a group that's quite antique . . .*'

'What?'

'*Half-naked, loving, natural and Greek.*' Joanna blushed slightly. 'Byron.'

'Him again! Pretty sexy type, wasn't he?'

'Yes, he was, as a matter of fact.'

'Like me,' said Desmond complacently, stroking Joanna through the sheet.

The next day, after lunch, there was a little embarrassed hesitation on the landing before they separated for the siesta. Then Desmond said to Robin, 'Why don't you go in Sally's room this time?' and a few moments later Robin and Joanna passed each other in the corridor wearing bathrobes and bashful smiles. The same thing happened the next day, and the day after that. They formed a silent, thoughtful group over the late-night coffee. The communal cuddle was a rather perfunctory ritual now: all had tasted headier pleasures in the afternoon. Afterwards they found it difficult to sleep in their hot, dark bedrooms.

'Des . . .'

'Mmm?'

'Have you ever, you know . . . ?'

'What?'

'Done it with a girl.'

After a longish pause, Desmond answered, 'I don't know.'

Robin sat up in his bed. 'Either you have or you haven't!'

'I tried once, but I don't think I did it properly.'

'What, you and Jo?'

'Good God, no!'

'Who then?'

'I've forgotten her name. It was years ago, I was camping, with the Scouts, in the Dales. These two local girls used to hang about the camp at night. Me and this other chap went for a walk with them one night. The one I was with suddenly said, "You can do me if you like."'

'Ye gods,' Robin breathed enviously.

'It was sopping wet on the ground, so we stood up against a tree. I kept slipping on the roots and I couldn't see a damned thing. Afterwards she said, "Well, I wouldn't give thee a badge for that, lad."'

Robin laughed aloud and gratefully.

'What about you?' Desmond enquired.

Robin was glum again. 'Never.'

'What made you ask?'

'These afternoons with Sal. It's driving me mad.'

'I know. We nearly went the whole way today.'

'So did we.'

'We'd better give it some serious thought.'

'I think about it all the time.'

'I mean precautions.'

'Oh. Yes, I suppose it would be risky.'

'Risky!'

'You didn't bring any with you, I suppose, what d'you call 'em . . .'

'French letters?'

'That's right.'

'Me?'

'Well, someone of your experience . . .'

'What experience?'

'In the Scouts.'

'Don't be daft.'

'What shall we do, then?'

'We could try the local shops.'

'Hmm.' Robin was doubtful. 'Catholic country, you know. Probably illegal. Anyway, what are they called in Spanish?'

'Let's look in the phrase book.'

'Good idea.' Robin jumped out of bed and turned on the light. Together they bent their heads over *The Holidaymaker's Spanish Phrase Book.*

'What will it be under?'

'Try "The Chemist's Shop", or "At the Barber's".'

'Oh yes,' said Robin bitterly, after a few minutes' perusal. 'They find room for *"I have blisters on the soles of my feet"*, and

*"Please may I have a shampoo for a dry scalp"*, but when there's something you're actually likely to *need . . .'*

'Hang on,' said Desmond. 'We didn't look at "Consulting the Doctor". There's a sort of all-purpose phrase here which says, *"I have a pain in my . . ."* You don't think we could adapt that?'

'No.' Robin turned off the light and groped his way back to bed. Some time later he found himself staring into the light and the eyes of Desmond, who was shaking him urgently, hissing the words *'New Statesman'*.

'Uh?'

'Your *New Statesman*. It has Family Planning ads in the back.'

Robin was suddenly wide awake. 'Des, you're a genius,' he said. And then: 'But there won't be time.'

'I worked it out. If we send off tomorrow, they should arrive in a week, or just over.'

'That's cutting it fine.'

'Well, have you got a better idea?'

Robin hadn't. They found an advertisement in the *New Statesman*, but it offered only a free catalogue. Not knowing the price or specifications of their requirements, they had some difficulty composing an order. But at last it was finished. In enclosing the money they agreed to err on the side of generosity. 'Let's tell them to keep the change,' said Robin. 'That should hurry things up.'

\* \* \*

Meanwhile, however, another conversation had been going on at the other end of the corridor which rendered these labours vain. The girls broke it to them the next morning on the beach.

'Jo and I had a serious talk last night,' said Sally. 'And we agreed that it's got to stop, before it's too late.'

'What's got to stop?' said Robin.

'Why?' said Desmond, who saw no point in pretending not to understand.

'Because it isn't right,' said Joanna.

'We all know it isn't,' said Sally.

The two boys were sulky and taciturn over lunch. Afterwards they went grimly to their room for the siesta, and the girls to theirs.

'Oh dear,' said Sally. 'I do hope this is not going to spoil the holiday.'

'What we need,' said Joanna sensibly, 'is a change of scenery. Let's go into Ibiza tomorrow.'

So the next day they took the bus into the town. There was a small crowd of people gathered on the quayside, watching a rather rakish-looking, black-painted yacht. Robin caught the name of a famous film star.

'Ooh!' said Sally. 'Let's wait and see if he comes ashore.'

They hung around for a while, but the famous film star did not appear. Once a well-developed young woman in a two-piece swimsuit stared haughtily at them for a few moments from a hatchway and then withdrew.

'No wonder he doesn't want to come ashore,' said Desmond.

'Let's go, I'm bored,' said Joanna.

They wandered round the old town, doing their best to avoid the gruesome cripples who begged on every street corner. They climbed up a succession of steep, smelly alleys festooned with washing, and found themselves on the parapet of a kind of fortress overlooking the harbour. Inside the fort was a little archaeological museum, with flints and shards and some coins and carvings. Joanna and Sally went to the Ladies. Sally emerged first, somewhat shaken by the experience, and found the boys poring over a glass display case.

'What have you found?'

Robin smirked. 'Take a look.'

The case contained a number of tiny, crudely fashioned clay figures, with grossly exaggerated sexual organs: huge phalluses, jutting breasts and grooved, distended bellies.

'Oh,' said Sally, after staring at them blankly for a while. 'Fancy putting things like that in a museum.'

'What is it?' said Joanna, joining them.

Desmond made room for her. 'Fertility whatnots,' he said.

'We don't seem to be able to get away from the subject, do we?' Sally said to Joanna, as they left the museum. The two boys were sniggering together behind them as they walked arm in arm down the hill.

For the rest of the day, and all the next day, Desmond and Robin kept together, leaving the girls to each other's company, implying that if that was how it was to be for the siesta, that was how it had better be all the time. The girls were well aware of this message, and it made them restive and unhappy. At dinner Robin and Desmond talked animatedly about the molecular structure of clay and its possible application to the dating of fertility whatnots, and in the *bodega* afterwards they pursued the same topic over Green Chartreuse. Two young Americans in violently checked Bermuda shorts asked politely if they might sit at the same table, for the bar was crowded, and were drawn into the discussion. Robin and Desmond described the treasures of the Ibiza museum in eloquent detail, while the two Americans grinned at the two girls.

'We can't go on like this,' said Sally that night.

'But we can't change our minds,' said Joanna. 'Can we?'

'I've been thinking,' said Sally, 'it would be different if we were engaged.'

'Yes,' said Joanna thoughtfully, 'it would, wouldn't it.'

So the next day they all got engaged. It was unofficial – they would wait till they got home to tell their parents – but it was quite properly done. Each girl chose a cheap ring, 'to be going on with', from a stall in the market, and wore it proudly on her third finger. In the evening they had a celebration dinner in a restaurant, and sentimentally held hands between courses. The two Americans, who happened to be in the same restaurant, noticed the rings and offered their congratulations.

'I'm ever so glad we decided to get engaged,' said Joanna to Desmond the following afternoon, 'aren't you, Des?'

'Oh yes.'

'Not just so we can siesta together?'

'Course not.'

'It's different, somehow, being definitely engaged. I mean, before, I was never quite sure whether we weren't just doing it for pleasure. But now I know it's for love.'

'Pleasure too.'

'Oh, yes, pleasure too. Oh Des!'

'Oh, Jo!'

'Goodness,' Sally murmured, averting her eyes, 'you look just like a fertility whatnot.'

'I feel like one,' said Robin.

It was not long before they all realised that they had not solved their problem, but merely raised the price of its solution. One fateful question hung over their waking hours, and their waking hours were many, for they discussed it late into the hot nights.

'Sal.'

'Yes?'

'We nearly did it today.'

'We nearly do it every day.'

'No, I mean really. I told Des, "If you want to, I couldn't stop you."'

'Gosh, what happened?'

'Well, he was ever so sweet. He said, "I'll give you ten to think it over," and went and sat on the other bed.'

'And?'

'When he'd finished counting, I'd sort of come round.'

'Didn't you wish you'd counted faster?' said Robin.

'Not really,' said Desmond. 'I sobered up myself. I began to think, what if Jo got pregnant? I mean, we're no nearer to getting married than we were last week.'

'It's about time those things came from the *New Statesman* place,' said Robin. 'There's not much time left.'

'Well, there aren't many days left now, anyhow,' said Joanna. 'It will be easier when we get back to England.'

'Yes, everything seems different abroad.'

'*What men call gallantry and gods adultery . . .*'

'It would be fornication, not adultery,' said Sally, who was getting rather tired of this quotation.

★ ★ ★

The next day, Desmond received a plain brown envelope in the mail and took it to his room, followed eagerly by Robin.

'There's nothing in it,' Desmond said grimly, 'I can feel.' He tore the envelope open and took out a letter and his cheque.

'Blast!'

'What do they say?'

'We regret that regulations prohibit us from conveying our goods to the Spanish Republic.'

'I told you,' said Robin. 'It's a Catholic country.'

'Fascist swine,' said Desmond. 'Inquisitors. Police state.' He worked himself up into a frenzy of anti-Spanish sentiment. 'Priest-mongers! Hypocrites!' He leaned out of the window and cried, 'Down with Franco! Up Sir Walter Raleigh!'

'I say, steady on,' said Robin.

The two Americans, who were passing in the street below, looked up wonderingly. Desmond waved to them.

'Rob,' he said over his shoulder, 'I wonder if those Yanks have any.'

'They've got things,' Sally said to Joanna that night.

'I know.'

'We must stick together, Jo.'

'Yes.'

'Why not?' said Robin. 'It's perfectly safe.'

'I'm sure it is,' said Sally. 'But . . .'

'But what?'

'Well, I think we should keep one thing for when we get married.'

'But we can't get married for years.'

'All the more reason.'


'I suppose you think I wouldn't respect you,' said Desmond. 'Afterwards.'

'Oh, no, Des, it's not that.'

'I'd respect you more. For having the courage of your convictions.'

'But I don't have any convictions. Just a feeling. That we'd regret it.'

Desmond sighed and rolled away from her. 'You disappoint me, Jo,' he said.


'D'you think we're being unreasonable?' said Joanna that night.

'I think *they're* being unreasonable,' said Sally. 'After all, we've given in and given in.'

'You've got to draw the line somewhere.'

'Exactly.'

'I suppose it's different for a boy, though,' said Joanna.

'Rob', said Sally, 'says it's like holding your thumb against a running tap.'

Lying in the darkness, the two girls silently pondered this eloquent image. Joanna flapped her sheet to make a breeze. 'It seems hotter than ever,' she said.


\* \* \*

And so, as the holiday drew towards its close, tension increased and found relief in a debauch of talk. They no longer bothered to maintain the convention that each couple conducted its intimate life in private: they brought their common problem out into the open and discussed it – on the beach, at meals, over drinks – with a freedom and sophistication that amazed themselves. 'I think we're all agreed that there's no special virtue in virginity *qua* virginity,' Robin would say, with the air of a chairman who sensed that he had the feeling of the meeting, and they would all nod sagely in agreement. 'In fact, I think one could safely say that *some* sexual experience before marriage is positively desirable.'

'Yes, I agree,' said Sally, 'in principle. I mean the first time could be an awful shambles if neither of you knew what you were supposed to be doing, and why should the girl always be the innocent one? That's old hat.'

'But don't you think,' said Joanna, 'that it's a shame if there's nothing to look forward to when you get married? I mean, if it's just legalising what's already happened?'

'The trouble is,' said Desmond, 'that we got attached to the people we want to marry before we had a chance to get sexual experience with anyone else.'

'You know, Des, that's rather neatly put,' said Sally.

It was like old times again: the relaxed camaraderie of their undergraduate days was restored. There was again a lively four-pointed discussion over coffee late at night. But it was not until the penultimate night of their holiday that they faced the fact that there was only one solution to their dilemma.

They were sitting on the beds in the girls' room, flushed and bright-eyed from the drinks they had consumed in the course of the evening (rather more than usual, for they were getting reckless with their pesetas), when Desmond put it to them.

'It seems to me,' he said, swirling the coffee dregs in his tooth mug, 'that if we all want to have the experience, but we don't want to anticipate marriage, and we don't want to go with tarts or gigolos—'

'Certainly not,' said Sally.

'What a revolting idea,' said Joanna.

'Then there's only one possibility left.'

'Swap, you mean?' said Robin.

'Mmm,' said Desmond. To his surprise, nobody laughed. He glanced swiftly round the group. Their eyes did not meet his, but beneath lowered lids they gleamed with the sly wantonness of children who have been left alone together, for too long, in an empty house, on a wet afternoon.

Some two hours later, Sally knocked at the door of the room she shared with Joanna. Robin opened it almost immediately, pale-faced and staring wildly.

'Have you finished?' Sally whispered.

He nodded jerkily, and stood aside to admit her. She avoided his eyes. 'Goodnight,' she said, and almost pushed him into the corridor. He was still standing there, staring at her, as she closed the door. Inside the room, Joanna was sobbing quietly into her pillow.

'Oh God,' said Sally, 'don't tell me you did it?'

Joanna sat up. 'Didn't you, then?'

'No.'

'Oh, thank *heavens!*' Joanna collapsed into renewed tears. 'Neither did we.'

'What are you crying about, then?'

'I thought you and Des . . . You were such a long time.'

'We were waiting for *you*. Des was frantic.'

'Poor Des!'

'I wonder how you can stand him.'

'Rob was *beastly*.'

'Was he?' Sally sounded pleased.

'Oh Sal, what happened to us? How could we ever dream of doing anything so awful?'

'I don't know,' said Sally, getting into bed. 'Perhaps it's this place. Sultry and adultery and all that.'

'You said it wasn't adultery,' Joanne sniffed.

'It would have been jolly near it this time,' said Sally.

\* \* \*

When Robin returned to his room, Desmond was smoking in the darkness. Robin silently took off his robe and got into bed.

'All right?' said Desmond, clearing his throat.

'Yes,' replied Robin. 'And you?'

'Oh, fine.' He added after a pause, 'I meant, you got on all right?'

'Yes. That's what I thought you meant.'

'Oh.'

'Is that what you thought *I* meant when you said, "Fine"?'

'Yes.'

'That's what I thought. What I meant.'

'Ah.' Desmond stubbed out his cigarette. ''Night then.'

'Goodnight.'

They turned and faced their respective walls, wide awake and racked with jealousy and hatred.

Next morning they rose, dressed and shaved in a hostile silence. Each surreptitiously disposed of an unopened packet of contraceptives before going down to breakfast.

The meal was strained. Joanna and Sally, secure in the knowledge that nothing irreparable had happened the previous night, were inclined to make light of the whole affair. It never occurred to them that Robin and Desmond had not been taken into each other's confidence. To them the boys' behaviour seemed merely boorish and unsporting; but to the boys the levity of Joanna and Sally seemed heartless and depraved. When, at length, Joanna indulged in her favourite quotation, Desmond leaned across the table and slapped her face, hard and resoundingly. A sudden hush fell over the dining room. A young waiter fled, rattling crockery, to the kitchen. Joanna whimpered, nursing her flushed cheek, her incredulous eyes swamped with tears.

'Des!' Sally exclaimed. 'What a foul thing to do!'

'You encouraged her,' Robin accused.

Joanna rose unsteadily to her feet. Sally scrambled to assist her. 'You make me sick,' she hissed at Robin and Desmond. 'You know what's the matter with you? You're both impotent, so you try to prove your virility by hitting.' Impotent? *Both* impotent? Desmond and Robin looked at each other and illumination flashed between them.

'Jo!'

'Sal! Wait!'

They rose to pursue the girls, but a little Spaniard with a moustache interposed himself and inflated his chest. The proprietress bustled in with the young waiter in tow, grasping a saucepan, like a weapon, in her hand. The girls disappeared upstairs. Desmond and Robin decided to leave the premises. As they emerged into the street, the two Americans passed in a hired pony and trap. They winked and raised their eyebrows interrogatively. One grasped his bicep and flexed his forearm; the other formed a circle with his finger and thumb.

'Oh, go to hell,' said Robin.

The quarrel was soon made up, and the misunderstanding erased. That afternoon, the last of their holiday, they took their siestas as before, Desmond with Joanna and Sally with Robin. Three months later, Desmond and Joanna got married rather suddenly, Sally being the bridesmaid and Robin the best man. A few weeks later the roles were reversed.

The two couples continued to take their summer holidays together. Having three children apiece, of approximately the same ages, they found the arrangement worked well. Now these children are themselves grown up, and fly off on package holidays for the under-30s whose advertising copy is a positive incitement to sexual promiscuity. As for Des and Rob and Jo and Sal, they have all become enthusiastic golfers in middle age, and spend their summer holidays exploring the links on the east coast of Scotland, where the climate is generally described as 'bracing'.

# Hotel des Boobs

'Hotel des Pins!' said Harry. 'More like Hotel des Boobs.'

'Come away from that window,' said Brenda. 'Stop behaving like a Peeping Tom.'

'What d'you mean, a Peeping Tom?' said Harry, continuing to squint down at the pool area through the slats of their bedroom shutters. 'A Peeping Tom is someone who interferes with someone else's privacy.'

'This is a private hotel.'

'Hotel des Tits. Hotel des Bristols. Hey, that's not bad!' He turned his head to flash a grin across the room. 'Hotel Bristols, plural. Geddit?'

If Brenda got it, she wasn't impressed. Harry resumed his watch. 'I'm not interfering with anyone's privacy,' he said. 'If they don't want people to look at their tits, why don't they cover them up?'

'Well go and look, then. Don't peep. Go down to the pool and have a good look.' Brenda dragged a comb angrily through her hair. 'Hold an inspection.'

'You're going to have to go topless, you know, Brenda, before this holiday's over.'

Brenda snorted derisively.

'Why not? You've nothing to be ashamed of.' He turned his head again to leer encouragingly at her. 'You've still got a fine pair.'

'Thanks very much, I'm sure,' said Brenda. 'But I intend to keep them covered as per usual.'

'When in Rome,' said Harry.

'This isn't Rome, it's the Côte d'Azur.'

'Côte des Tits,' said Harry. 'Côte des Knockers.'

'If I'd known you were going to go on like this,' said Brenda, 'I'd never have come here.'

For years Harry and Brenda had taken family holidays every summer in Guernsey, where Brenda's parents lived. But now that the children were grown up enough to make their own arrangements, they had decided to have a change. Brenda had always wanted to see the South of France, and they felt they'd earned the right to treat themselves for once. They were quite comfortably off, now that Brenda, a recent graduate of the Open University, had a full-time job as a teacher. It had caused an agreeable stir in the managerial canteen at Barnard Castings when Harry dropped the name of their holiday destination in among the Benidorms and Palmas, the Costas of this and that, whose merits were being debated by his colleagues.

'The French Riviera, Harry?'

'Yes, a little hotel near Saint-Raphael. Brenda got the name out of a book.'

'Going up in the world, aren't we?'

'Well, it *is* pricey. But we thought, well, why not be extravagant, while we're still young enough to enjoy it.'

'Enjoy eyeing all those topless birds, you mean.'

'Is that right?' said Harry, with an innocence that was not entirely feigned. Of course he knew in theory that in certain parts of the Mediterranean women sunbathed topless on the beach, and he had seen pictures of the phenomenon in his secretary's daily newspaper, which he filched regularly for the sake of such illustrations. But the reality had been a shock. Not so much the promiscuous, anonymous breastbaring of the beach, as the more intimate and socially complex nudity around the hotel pool. What made the pool different, and more disturbing, was that the women who lay half-naked around its perimeter all day were the same as those you saw immaculately dressed for dinner in the evening, or nodded and smiled politely at in the lobby, or exchanged small talk about the weather with in the bar. And since Brenda found the tree-shaded pool, a few miles inland, infinitely preferable to the heat and glare and crowdedness of the beach (not to mention the probable pollution of the sea), it became the principal theatre of Harry's initiation into the new code of mammary manners.

Harry – he didn't mind admitting it – had always had a thing about women's breasts. Some men went for legs, or bums, but Harry had always been what the boys at Barnard's called a tit-fancier. 'You were weaned too early,' Brenda used to say, a diagnosis that Harry accepted with a complacent grin. He always glanced, a simple reflex action, at the bust of any sexually interesting female that came within his purview, and had spent many idle moments speculating about the shapes that were concealed beneath their sweaters, blouses and brassieres. It was disconcerting, to say the least, to find this harmless pastime rendered totally redundant under the Provençal sun. He had scarcely begun to assess the figures of the women at the Hotel des Pins before they satisfied his curiosity to the last pore. Indeed, in most cases he saw them half-naked before he met them, as it were, socially. The snooty Englishwoman, for instance, mother of twin boys and wife to the tubby stockbroker never seen without yesterday's *Financial Times* in his hand and a smug smile on his face. Or the female half of the German couple who worshipped the sun with religious zeal, turning and anointing themselves according to a strict timetable and with the aid of a quartz alarm clock. Or the deeply tanned brunette of a certain age whom Harry had privately christened Carmen Miranda, because she spoke an eager and rapid Spanish, or it might have been Portuguese, into the cordless telephone which the waiter Antoine brought to her at frequent intervals.

Mrs Snooty had hardly any breasts at all when she was lying down, just boyish pads of what looked like muscle, tipped with funny little turned-up nipples that quivered like the noses of two small rodents when she stood up and moved about. The German lady's breasts were perfect cones, smooth and firm as if turned on a lathe, and never seemed to change their shape whatever posture she adopted; whereas Carmen Miranda's were like two brown satin bags filled with a viscous fluid that ebbed and flowed across her ribcage in continual motion as she turned and twisted restlessly on her mattress, awaiting the next phone call from her absent lover. And this morning there were a pair of teenage girls down by the pool whom Harry hadn't seen before, reclining side by side, one in green bikini pants and the other in yellow, regarding their recently acquired breasts, hemispheres smooth and flawless as jelly moulds, with the quiet satisfaction of housewives watching scones rise.

'There are two newcomers today,' said Harry, 'or should I say, four.'

'Are you coming down?' said Brenda, at the door. 'Or are you going to spend the morning peering through the shutters?'

'I'm coming. Where's my book?' He looked around the room for his Jack Higgins paperback.

'You're not making much progress with it, are you?' said Brenda sarcastically. 'I think you ought to move the bookmark every day, for appearance's sake.' A book was certainly basic equipment for discreet boobwatching down by the pool: something to peer over, or round, something to look up from, as if distracted by a sudden noise or movement, at the opportune moment, just as the bird a few yards away slipped her costume off her shoulders, or rolled on to her back. Another essential item was a pair of sunglasses, as dark as possible, to conceal the precise direction of one's gaze. For there was, Harry realised, a protocol involved in toplessness. For a man to stare at, or even let his eyes rest for a measurable span of time upon, a bared bosom would be bad form, because it would violate the fundamental principle upon which the whole practice was based, namely, that there was nothing noteworthy about it, that it was the most natural, neutral thing in the world. (Antoine was particularly skilled in managing to serve his female clients cold drinks, or take their orders for lunch, stooping low over their prone figures, without seeming to notice their nakedness.) Yet this principle was belied by another, which confined toplessness to the pool and its margins. As soon as they moved on to the terrace, or into the hotel itself, the women covered their upper halves. Did bare bosoms gain and lose erotic value in relation to arbitrary territorial zones? Did the breast eagerly gazed upon, fondled and nuzzled by husband or lover in the privacy of the bedroom become an object of indifference, a mere anatomical protuberance no more interesting than an elbow or kneecap, on the concrete rim of the swimming pool? Obviously not. The idea was absurd. Harry had little doubt that, like himself, all the men present, including Antoine, derived considerable pleasure and stimulation from the toplessness of most of the women, and it was unlikely that the women themselves were unaware of this fact. Perhaps they found it exciting, Harry speculated, to expose themselves knowing that the men must not betray any sign of arousal; and their own menfolk might share, in a vicarious, proprietorial way, in this excitement. Especially if one's own wife was better endowed than some of the others. To intercept the admiring and envious glance of another man at your wife's boobs, to think silently to yourself, *'Yes, all right, matey, you can look, as long as it's not too obvious, but only I'm allowed to touch 'em, see?'* That might be very exciting.

Lying beside Brenda at the poolside, dizzy from the heat and the consideration of these puzzles and paradoxes, Harry was suddenly transfixed by an arrow of perverse desire: to see his wife naked, and lust after her, through the eyes of other men. He rolled over on to his stomach and put his mouth to Brenda's ear.

'If you'll take your top off,' he whispered, 'I'll buy you that dress we saw in Saint-Raphael. The one for twelve hundred francs.'

\* \* \*

The author had reached this point in his story, which he was writing seated at an umbrella-shaded table on the terrace over-looking the hotel pool, using a fountain pen and ruled foolscap, as was his wont, and having accumulated many cancelled and rewritten pages, as was also his wont, when without warning a powerful wind arose. It made the pine trees in the hotel grounds shiver and hiss, raised wavelets on the surface of the pool, knocked over several umbrellas, and whirled the leaves of the author's manuscript into the air. Some of these floated back on to the terrace, or the margins of the pool, or into the pool itself, but many were funnelled with astonishing speed high into the air, above the trees, by the hot breath of the wind. The author staggered to his feet and gaped unbelievingly at the leaves of foolscap rising higher and higher, like escaped kites, twisting and turning in the sun, white against the azure sky. It was like the visitation of some god or daemon, a Pentecost in reverse, drawing words away instead of imparting them. The author felt raped. The female sunbathers around the pool, as if similarly conscious, covered their naked breasts as they stood and watched the whirling leaves of paper recede into the distance. Faces were turned towards the author, smiles of sympathy mixed with *Schadenfreude*. Bidden by the sharp voice of their mother, the English twins scurried round the pool's edge collecting up loose sheets, and brought them with doggy eagerness back to their owner. The German, who had been in the pool at the time of the wind, came up with two sodden pages, covered with weeping longhand, held between finger and thumb, and laid them carefully on the author's table to dry. Pierre, the waiter, presented another sheet on his tray. '*C'est le petit mistral,*' he said with a *moue* of commiseration. '*Quel dommage!*' The author thanked them mechanically, his eyes still on the airborne pages, now mere specks in the distance, sinking slowly down into the pine woods. Around the hotel the air was quite still again. Slowly the guests returned to their loungers and mattresses. The women discreetly uncovered their bosoms, renewed the application of Ambre Solaire, and resumed the pursuit of the perfect tan.

'Simon! Jasper!' said the Englishwoman. 'Why don't you go for a walk in the woods and see if you can find any more of the gentleman's papers?'

'Oh, no,' said the author urgently. 'Please don't bother. I'm sure they're miles away by now. And they're really not important.'

'No bother,' said the Englishwoman. 'They'll enjoy it.'

'Like a treasure hunt,' said her husband, 'or rather, paper-chase.' He chuckled at his own joke. The boys trotted off obediently into the woods. The author retired to his room, to await the return of his wife, who had missed all the excitement, from Saint-Raphael.

'I've bought the most darling little dress,' she announced as she entered the room. 'Don't ask me how much it cost.'

'Twelve hundred francs?'

'Good God, no, not as much as that. Seven hundred and fifty, actually. What's the matter, you look funny?'

'We've got to leave this hotel.'

He told her what had happened.

'I shouldn't worry,' said his wife. 'Those little brats probably won't find any more sheets.'

'Oh yes they will. They'll regard it as a challenge, like the Duke of Edinburgh Award. They'll comb the pine woods for miles around. And if they find anything, they're sure to read it.'

'They wouldn't understand.'

'Their parents would. Imagine Mrs Snooty finding her nipples compared to the nose tips of small rodents.'

The author's wife spluttered with laughter. 'You are a fool,' she said.

'It wasn't my fault,' he protested. 'The wind sprang out of nowhere.'

'An act of God?'

'Precisely.'

'Well, I don't suppose He approved of that story. I can't say I cared much for it myself. How was it going to end?'

The author's wife knew the story pretty well as far as he had got with it, because he had read it out to her in bed the previous night.

'Brenda accepts the bribe to go topless.'

'I don't think she would.'

'Well, she does. And Harry is pleased as Punch. He feels that he and Brenda have finally liberated themselves, joined the sophisticated set. He imagines himself telling the boys back at Barnard Castings about it, making them ribaldly envious. He gets such a hard-on that he has to lie on his stomach all day.'

'Tut, tut!' said his wife. 'How crude.'

'He can't wait to get to bed that night. But just as they're retiring, they separate for some reason I haven't worked out yet, and Harry goes up to their room first. She doesn't come at once, so Harry gets ready for bed, lies down, and falls asleep. He wakes up two hours later and finds Brenda is still missing. He is alarmed and puts on his dressing gown and slippers to go in search of her. Just at that moment, she comes in. *Where the hell have you been?* he says. She has a peculiar look on her face, goes to the fridge in their room and drinks a bottle of Perrier water before she tells him her story. She says that Antoine intercepted her downstairs to present her with a bouquet. It seems that each week all the male staff of the hotel take a vote on which female guest has the shapeliest breasts, and Brenda has come top of the poll. The bouquet was a mark of their admiration and respect. She is distressed because she left it behind in Antoine's room.'

'Antoine's room?'

'Yes, he coaxed her into seeing his room, a little chalet in the woods, and gave her a drink, and one thing led to another, and she ended up letting him make love to her.'

'How improbable.'

'Not necessarily. Taking off her bra in public might have released some dormant streak of wantonness in Brenda that Harry had never seen before. Anyway, she's rather drunk and quite shameless. She taunts him with graphic testimony to Antoine's skill as a lover, and says he is much better endowed than Harry.'

'Worse and worse,' said the author's wife.

'At which point Harry slaps her.'

'Oh, nice. Very nice.'

'Brenda half undresses and crawls into bed. A couple of hours later, she wakes up. Harry is standing by the window staring down at the empty pool, a ghostly blue by the light of the moon. Brenda gets out of bed, comes across and touches him on the arm. *Come to bed*, she says. *It wasn't true what I told you.* He turns his face slowly towards her. *Not true?* he says. *No, I made it up*, she says. *I went and sat in the car for two hours with a bottle of wine, and I made it up. Why?* he says. *I don't know why*, she says. *To teach you a lesson, I suppose. I was fed up with you. But it was a stupid idea. Come to bed.* But Harry just shakes his head and turns back to stare out of the window. *You always used to say size didn't matter*, he says. *Well, it doesn't, not to me*, she says. *I told you, I made it all up.* Harry just shakes his head disbelievingly, gazing down at the blue, breastless margins of the pool. That's how the story was going to end: "he gazed down at the blue, breastless margins of the pool."'

As he spoke these words, the author was himself standing at the window, looking down at the hotel pool from which all the guests had departed to change for dinner. Only the solitary figure of Pierre moved among the umbrellas and tables, collecting discarded bathing towels and soiled teatrays.

'Hmm,' said the author's wife.

'Harry's fixation on women's breasts, you see,' said the author, 'has been displaced by an anxiety about his own body from which he will never be free.'

'Yes, I see that. I'm not totally without critical acumen, you know.' The author's wife came to the window and looked down. 'Poor Pierre,' she said. 'He wouldn't dream of making a pass at any of us women. He's obviously gay.'

'Fortunately,' said the author, 'I hadn't got that far with my story when the wind scattered it all over the countryside. But you'd better get out the Michelin and find another hotel. I can't stand the thought of staying on here, on tenterhooks all the time in case one of the guests comes back from a walk in the woods with a compromising piece of fiction in their paws. What an extraordinary thing to happen.'

'You know,' said the author's wife. 'It's really a better story.'

'Yes,' said the author. 'I think I shall write it. I'll call it "Tit for Tat".'

'No, call it "Hotel des Boobs",' said the author's wife. 'Theirs and yours.'

'What about yours?'

'Just leave them out of it, please.'

Much later that night, when they were in bed and just dropping off to sleep, the author's wife said:

'You don't really wish I would go topless, do you?'

'No, of course not?' said the author. But he didn't sound entirely convinced, or convincing.

# Pastoral

Dah *dah* dah, dah *dah* dah, dada dada dada . . . I never hear the opening strains of the 'Shepherd's Song' from Beethoven's Pastoral Symphony without remembering my scheme to embrace the Virgin Mary. That is to say, Dympna Cassidy, who was impersonating the Virgin Mary at the time. The time was one Christmas in the early 1950s, and the occasion a Nativity play I produced for the Youth Club of Our Lady of Perpetual Succour, in South London. And when I say produced, I mean I wrote the piece, directed it, cast it, acted in it, designed the set for it and of course chose the music for it. The only thing I didn't do for it was sew the costumes. My loyal mother and resentful sisters were pressed into performing that task.

It must sound as if I was already stagestruck, but in fact I wasn't when I embarked on the project. I was in the sixth form at St Aloysius' Catholic Grammar School, studying English, French, Latin and Economics, and intended to read Law at university, with the ambition of becoming a barrister (an idea implanted by my father, who was a solicitor's chief clerk, and had set his heart on my becoming a star of the legal profession). I never expected to end up as a director of stage musicals anywhere from Scunthorpe to Sydney – mostly touring productions of golden oldies like *Oklahoma!* and *The King and I*. I did direct a new musical in the West End a few years ago, but you probably never heard of it – it folded after three weeks. Still, I have great hopes of my new project, a musical version of *Antony and Cleopatra* called *Cleo!* I've written the book myself.

But I digress. Back to the Nativity play, *The Story of Christmas*, as it was rather unimaginatively entitled. I wanted to call it *The Fruit of the Womb*, but the parish priest, Father Stanislaus Lynch, wouldn't have it – the first of many battles we had over the play. He said my title was indecent. I pointed out that it was a quotation from the Hail Mary: 'and blessed is the fruit of thy womb, Jesus.' He said that, taken out of context, the words had a different effect. I said: 'What you mean is that *in* context they have no effect at all, because Catholics recite prayers in a mindless drone, without paying any attention to what they're saying. My play is designed to shock them out of their mental torpor, into a new awareness of what Christmas is all about – Incarnation.' I was a fluent and arrogant youth – at least in intellectual debate. In other areas of life, such as girls, I was less assured.

But Father Stan, as we called him, replied: 'That's all very well, but there'll have to be a poster advertising it. I won't have the word "womb" stuck up in my church porch. The Union of Catholic Mothers wouldn't like it.' At home I complained bitterly about this example of philistine ecclesiastical censorship, until one of my sisters said that *Fruit of the Womb* reminded her of 'Fruit of the Loom', in those days a well-known trade mark for cotton underwear, and I decided to abandon the title without further resistance.

Dah *dah* dah, dah *dah* dah . . . There were other pieces of music in *The Story of Christmas*, played while the scenery was being changed behind the curtain, and setting the mood for the next scene. I chose Gounod's 'Ave Maria' for the Annunciation, a theme from Rimsky-Korsakov's *Scheherazade* for the Three Kings, and the 'Ride of the Valkyries' for the Flight into Egypt. My father had a decent collection of classical music on 78s, and used to let me play them on our radiogram, a walnut-veneered monolith that stood in the bay window of the front parlour. But it's the 'Shepherd's Song', only the 'Shepherd's Song', that triggers memories of the play, and of Dympna Cassidy. I chose it, of course, to introduce the scene where the shepherds of Bethlehem come to venerate the infant Jesus, but it spread into other parts of the play in the course of rehearsals.

\* \* \*

It all started one Sunday evening early in November, at a youth club hop. Father Stan and I were sitting on a pair of folding chairs on the edge of the dance floor, if one might so dignify the dusty, splintering floorboards of the parish hall, watching the couples shuffling round to Nat King Cole groaning 'Too Young' from a portable record-player.

I was sitting down because I didn't dance, couldn't dance, pretended I didn't want to dance, though truly it was a reluctance to look silly while learning to dance that made me a wallflower. I attended these events on the pretext of being Secretary of the Youth Club Committee: drawn by a secret need to behold Dympna Cassidy, exquisite torture though it was to watch her swaying in the arms of some other youth. Fortunately most of the boys in the club were as shy as I was, and the girls were compelled much of the time to dance with each other, as Dympna was doing with her friend Pauline that evening to the syrupy strains of 'Too Young'; and even when she had a male partner, club protocol prohibited close contact between dancing couples. That was why Father Stan was there: to make sure light was always visible between them.

> They say that we are much too young,
> Too young to really be in love . . .

Not that I was in love with Dympna Cassidy. That was the problem.

She was beautiful and buxom, with jade green eyes and copper-coloured hair, which, freshly washed for social occasions, surrounded her head in a shimmering haze of natural curls. Her complexion was a glowing, translucent white, like the surface of a fine alabaster statue, and her underlip had a delicious pout. When she smiled two dimples appeared in her cheeks which I associated with her name, her first name. Cassidy was rather lacking in poetic resonance, but Dympna – it was eloquent not only of her dimples, but of her whole person. The syllables had a soft, yielding, pneumatic quality that I imagined her body would possess when clasped in an embrace. And how I longed to embrace it! How I yearned to squeeze that voluptuous form like a cushion against my chest, and press my lips on the pouting perfection of her mouth, in the manner I had observed in a thousand cinematic love scenes. But I didn't love Dympna Cassidy. Nor was I prepared to pretend that I did. And in that time and place the only way you would get to kiss a girl like her was to do one or the other. That is to say, I would have had to declare myself publicly as her steady boyfriend.

And here I have to make a rather shameful confession: I thought I would be lowering myself if I courted Dympna Cassidy. It wasn't simply that she came from the wrong side of the tracks, though she did; her large and slightly raffish family lived in a tenement flat on a council estate, whereas we owned our own home, a dignified Victorian terraced house, with a flight of steps leading up to the front door. It wasn't that she dropped her aitches occasionally, and tended to elide the middle consonant of 'butter' and 'better'. I could have lived with these handicaps if Dympna Cassidy had possessed some qualities of mind to compare with the attractions of her body. But her mind was conspicuously empty. There was nothing to be found in it except a few popular songs, the names of film stars, fashion notes, and anecdotes about her teachers. She attended a technical school, having failed the 11-plus examination in which I had distinguished myself, and was following what was called a commercial course. She was being trained to be a shorthand typist, though her own inclination was to be a sales assistant in a dress shop. I knew all this because I took the opportunity to chat to her – outside church after Sunday Mass, while clearing up the parish hall after a youth club evening, or during one of the club's occasional rambles through the Kent countryside. I could tell that Dympna was interested in me: intrigued and attracted by the slightly foppish air I cultivated when out of school uniform, my long hair, green corduroy jacket and mustard waistcoat. I was aware that she had attached herself to no other boy, though she had many admirers in the parish. I felt sure that she would reciprocate, if I would only make the first move.

But I hung back. My future was clearly marked out for me, and Dympna Cassidy had no place in it: study, examinations, honours, prizes; years of effort and self-denial ultimately rewarded by a distinguished legal career. Dympna's kind had a totally different attitude to life: leave school as soon as you could, get a job however repetitive and banal, and live for the hours of leisure and recreation, for dancing, shopping, going to the pictures, 'having a good time'. Consuming one's youth in a splurge of thoughtless, superficial pleasure, before relapsing into a dull, domesticated adulthood just like one's parents, struggling to bring up a family on inadequate means. Becoming involved with Dympna would, I was certain, drag me down into that abyss. I swear that I thought one kiss would do it, one kiss and I would be set on a course leading to a premature and imprudent marriage. And marriage would not be kind to Dympna Cassidy. You could see what she would look like in twenty years' time by looking at her mother: a sagging bosom, a waist thickened by childbearing, and hollowed cheeks where the back teeth were missing. Dympna would never again be as beautiful as she was now, so I told myself gloomily, watching her leading Pauline in the foxtrot, chattering away inanely about a pair of shoes that she had seen in a shop window. This topic seemed to engage their interest for the duration of the set; they were still talking about it every time they rotated past me and Father Stan.

'You know Mrs Noonan who teaches in the Infants,' he said suddenly. I admitted that I did: she had taught me ten years earlier. 'And you know she puts on a Nativity play every Christmas, with the children. Well, she's got to go into hospital next week for an operation, and she'll be on convalescent leave until January. I've been thinking, wouldn't it be a fine thing if the youth club took on the job for this year? The Nativity play, I mean. It would be good to have something a little more ... grown up, for once. Something the young people of the parish could relate to. D'you think you might be able to organise something, Simon?'

'All right.'

'Well, that's grand,' said Father Stan, somewhat taken aback by the speed of my assent. 'Are you sure you've got time? I know they work you very hard at St Aloysius.'

'I'll manage, Father. Leave it to me.'

'Well, that's very good of you. I'll see if the Catholic Truth Society publish a suitable play. I don't think the one Mrs Noonan uses would be quite the ticket.'

'I'll write the play myself.'

As soon as he had mentioned the Nativity play a tableau had formed in my mind's eye: Dympna Cassidy as Our Lady, stunningly beautiful, her copper filigree hair shining like a halo in the footlights, and myself as St Joseph, supporting her on the road to Bethlehem, my arm round her shoulders, or even her waist. I had found the perfect alibi for getting into close physical contact with Dympna Cassidy without incurring any moral or emotional obligations.

'You'd have to show me the script before it's performed, just to make sure there's no heresy.' Father Stan exposed his irregular, nicotine-stained teeth in a wolfish grin.

I wrote the play, believe it or not, over two weekends. I didn't bother with auditions, partly because there wasn't time, and partly because nobody would have turned up for them. There was no thespian tradition at the Youth Club of our Lady of Perpetual Succour. I picked out the likeliest members of the club for my cast and, as we say in the profession, made offers without asking them to read. Naturally I approached

Dympna Cassidy first. When I told her I wanted her to play the Virgin Mary she went pink with pleasure, but shook her head and bit her underlip and said that she had never acted in her life. I told her not to worry. I had some experience of acting in school plays, and I would help her. I looked forward to intimate coaching sessions in the front parlour at home, with the radiogram providing some suitable background music. Dah *dah* dah, dah *dah* dah . . . Did I already have that piece of music in mind?

I deferred showing Father Stan the script on the grounds that we were continually revising it in the course of rehearsals. But eventually he got suspicious and borrowed a copy from another member of the cast, and there was the most almighty row. He came round to our house one evening, fortunately when my parents were out, grasping the rolled-up script in his fist like a baton. He waved it furiously in my face. 'What's the meaning of this filth? What do you mean by soiling the spotless purity of our Blessed Mother?'

I knew at once that he was referring to the stage direction at the end of Act 1, Sc i: '*JOSEPH and MARY embrace*'.

Admittedly there wasn't a great deal of biblical authority for this scene. It was an imaginative attempt to evoke the life of Mary when betrothed to Joseph, and before she had any idea that she was to become the Mother of God. I was aiming at a contemporary style in my play – 'relevance', it would have been called a decade later. No pious platitudes and biblical archaisms, but colloquial speech and natural behaviour, that modern teenagers could relate to. I imagined Mary as a rather merry, high-spirited, even skittish young girl at this stage of her life, engaged to an older and rather serious man. I wrote a scene in which Mary calls in at Joseph's carpentry shop and tries to persuade him to go for a walk. Joseph refuses, he has a job to finish, and there is a kind of lovers' tiff, which is soon made up. And their reconciliation is sealed with a kiss.

Several members of the cast questioned the propriety of this scene at the first read-through. But I argued that it was natural behaviour between an engaged couple who didn't at that stage know that they were going to bring the Messiah into the world. Dympna herself didn't contribute to this discussion. She kept her eyes down and her lips closed. I think she had a good idea of the real motivation for the scene.

After a couple more read-throughs, I started blocking out the moves, starting from the top, but I found that when I came to the curtain line of Act 1, Sc. i –

JOSEPH: Mary, I can never be cross with you for long.
MARY: Nor I with you

– my nerve failed me. I simply said: 'Then Joseph and Mary embrace, and the curtain comes down.'

'Aren't you going to rehearse the kiss?' said Magda Vernon, who had volunteered to be Stage Manager. She was an odd girl, tall and skinny, with glasses that kept falling off her snub nose, and spiky black hair that stuck out in all directions, as if she had just got out of bed. She favoured long dark-hued sweaters that she pulled cruelly out of shape, tugging the hem down low over her hips, and stretching the sleeves so that they covered her hands like mittens, as though she were trying to hide herself in the garment. It was rumoured that she had had some kind of nervous breakdown, and tried to run away from home, and that her parents made her join the youth club so that she would become more normal. But she didn't seem to enjoy it much. The Nativity play was the first event that had aroused the slightest flicker of interest in her. She had supported me in the discussion about the propriety of the embrace, for which I was grateful. But now I wished she would not interfere.

'There isn't time to rehearse everything at this stage,' I said. 'Could we move on to Scene Two?' But the next time we ran the first scene, I stopped it again just short of the final kiss.

'Shouldn't you decide what kind of a kiss it's going to be?' Magda insisted. 'I mean, who kisses who? And is it a kiss on the lips or on the cheek?'

'It'd better be on the cheek,' said the boy playing Herod, 'or Father Stan will have a fit.' There was a general titter.

'I really haven't thought about it,' I lied, having thought of little else for days. 'I think we should leave it till we have the costumes.'

Later, when the cast had gone home, and Magda and I were alone, going through a list of props that would be required, she gave me an arch look: 'I don't believe you know how to.'

'How to what?'

'How to kiss a girl. I'll teach you if you like.'

'I can manage perfectly well on my own, thank you.'

But later, walking home in the cold December night, I rather regretted having turned down the offer, and mentally rehearsed various strategies for reviving it. But the very next day Father Stan exploded, the first scene of my play was scrapped, and I had no further pretext for requesting Magda's tuition.

So I never did get to embrace Dympna Cassidy. I got my arm round her waist on the road to Bethlehem, but she was wearing so many layers of clothing in that scene that it was no great tactile experience. By this time, in any case, I'd rather lost sexual interest in Dympna, and was much more preoccupied with her shortcomings as an actress. The manic, obsessive quest for perfection that possesses those who make plays had me in thrall. Dympna kept forgetting her lines. And when she remembered she delivered them in a flat and barely audible voice. If I criticised her she sulked and said that she'd never asked to be in my stupid play anyway. The only thing to be said for her was that she looked sensational. So what I did was to cut her lines to the bone and make her part consist mostly of silent action with background music. I noticed that she liked the 'Shepherd's Song', and would hum it to herself when she was in a good mood, so I decided to use it as a kind of leitmotif, whenever Mary appeared. This required some nifty work from Magda in the wings – she had to operate the portable gramophone and act as prompter at the same time – but it proved highly effective. I had stumbled on one of the primary resources of musical theatre: the reprise. No prizes for guessing what the audience was humming as they filed out of the parish hall. Our play was a hit. I walked Magda home afterwards, and we kissed in her front porch until our lips were sore.

Magda became my first girlfriend, until we both went to different universities the following year, and drifted apart. I read law as planned, but spent all my time mucking about in the Drama Society and the Opera Society, scraped a third-class degree, and to the great disgust of my father went straight into drama school. Curiously enough, Magda had been bitten by the same bug. She did theatre studies at university, became an ASM at various provincial reps and finally went into television, where she has done rather well as a production manager. We meet occasionally at showbiz occasions, and when we embrace each other, as showbiz people do when they meet, she always teases me by saying, 'Lips or cheek, darling?'

And Dympna? Well, she didn't become a typist or a shop assistant. And she didn't lose her figure or her teeth. Somebody spotted her potential as a photographic model, and she had a very successful run in the late 1950s, appearing on the front covers of several women's magazines, until the Jean Shrimpton look put her out of fashion. According to my mother, she married a rich businessman and retired from modelling. They live in a manor house near Newmarket and own a string of racehorses . . . I've been thinking I might write and ask them if they'd like to invest in *Cleo!*

# A Wedding to Remember

Emma Dobson, everyone who knew her agreed, was a young woman of strong character. 'Emma has a clear vision of her goals and priorities,' the headmistress of the sixth form college where she was Head Girl wrote in her final report, 'and she has the ability and determination to realise them.' This prediction proved accurate. She obtained a good 2.1 in Modern Languages at Bath University (a degree highly valued by employers because of its emphasis on current affairs rather than literature) and a Master's degree in Business Studies at Warwick. During the postgraduate course she lived conveniently and economically at home, a spacious modern house in the leafiest part of Solihull, and at the end of it was accepted for a fast-track training scheme by a national bank. She joined their Midland headquarters in Birmingham, where she was soon promoted to a responsible position in the Private Clients department. Her father, who was MD of a company which manufactured components for the car industry, gave her an interest-free loan to put down the deposit on a one-bedroom flat on the seventh floor of a new building overlooking a canal in the middle of the city, part of a system of drab industrial waterways recently transformed into an environment for leisure pursuits and stylish urban living.

At a course on new developments in financial services she met a young accountant called Neville Holloway, who also worked for a Birmingham-based firm, and started going out with him. He was a good-looking young man with dark brown eyes and beautiful white teeth which he frequently exposed in an engaging smile. Emma's teeth were a disappointment to her, small and irregular, so she had got into the habit of not smiling very much, but she was a natural blonde with otherwise pleasing features and a shapely size 12 figure. Catching sight of herself in a mirror standing or sitting beside Neville, she thought they made a handsome couple. After a while Neville moved into Emma's flat and contributed his fair share to the mortgage repayments and other expenses. They could walk to their respective workplaces, and at weekends they went jogging along the canal towpaths. They ate out a good deal in the numerous restaurants of varied ethnic character that had sprung up in the city centre. It was an agreeable life.

Emma's parents, who had grown up under the influence of a more puritanical moral code, did not really approve of their daughter's cohabitation with Neville, but they liked him well enough and reluctantly accepted that it was the way of young people nowadays, so they refrained from reproachful comment. One day, however, when the relationship was about three years old, Mrs Dobson, unable to contain her feelings any longer, asked Emma if she and Neville had any plans for the future. 'You mean marriage?' Emma asked. 'Well, yes, dear,' Mabel Dobson said nervously. 'As a matter of fact, I *have* been thinking about it lately,' Emma said, to her mother's great relief. Emma had always planned a future for herself in which marriage had its place. She and Neville had been living happily together long enough for her to feel comfortable about upgrading the relationship. Her mother's question was timely: it gave her a pretext for raising the matter with Neville, and she did so the very next evening.

He seemed surprised, and rather disconcerted. 'Aren't we quite happy as we are?' he said. 'Yes, but we can't go on like this indefinitely,' she said. 'I want to have children. That is, I don't positively want them at this moment,' she added scrupulously, 'but I know I will eventually, and if you leave it too late there are all kinds of health risks.' 'I take your point, Em,' Neville said, 'but there's no immediate hurry, is there?' 'It takes a long time to organise a wedding these days, especially the kind I want,' she said. 'What kind is that?' he asked. 'One to remember,' Emma said. 'For instance, I want to have the reception at Longstaffe Hall and I happen to know they're booked up for at least a year ahead for summer Saturdays.' Longstaffe Hall was an eighteenth-century country house in the green belt just outside Solihull, converted into a hotel. Neville had dined there with the Dobsons to celebrate Mrs Dobson's birthday, and was conscious of its attractions as a venue. 'Does it have to be a

Saturday – or in summer?' he said, smiling his engaging smile. 'Yes, it does,' Emma said, unsmiling. 'In June, before everyone you want to invite starts going on holiday.'

Emma had always promised herself a really memorable wedding, a sumptuous, extravagant, classic wedding, to mark the end of her single state. It would be a kind of reward for all the disciplined hard work that had made her life a success so far, and also a foil to it. She was aware that other people, her family and friends, especially girlfriends, thought of her as too disciplined for her own good, lacking warmth, incapable of spontaneity, tone-deaf to romance. Well, her wedding would show them they were wrong, that she was not indifferent to imagination, emotion and pleasure. But of course, being Emma, she brought to the preparation for this event the same methodical concentration, the same insistence on controlling every detail, that she had applied in other departments of her life. Outside business hours she made the planning of the wedding her mission, her passion, her all-consuming occupation.

Luckily, due to a cancellation, Longstaffe Hall was available on the last Saturday in June of the following year, a mere nine months away. Emma went with her parents to meet the hotel's Functions Manager and persuaded her father to book the entire place for their exclusive use for one day and night. She took home specimen menus and wine lists and made her choices with Neville, deferring to him only on the matter of drink. They drew up a guest list of a hundred and fifty people, not counting young children. When Frank Dobson made a rough calculation of the cost he was appalled. 'This is going to cost a small fortune,' he said to his wife. 'Well, she is our only daughter,' Mabel Dobson said, 'and you can afford it.' She said 'you' rather than 'we' because Mr Dobson was the sole breadwinner in the marriage, Mabel having retired permanently from her occupation as a dentist's receptionist shortly before giving birth to Emma, who was their only child. 'To think our wedding only cost five hundred pounds, according to your dad,' Frank mused. 'Even allowing for inflation that's a fraction of what this little affair will run to.' When he proposed to economise by serving sparkling white wine instead of champagne at the beginning of the reception, Emma did something she hadn't done since childhood: she threw a tantrum fit – accused him of being bent on spoiling the most important day of her life by his incredible meanness, in a voice that rose in pitch until it was almost a shriek and dissolved into broken-hearted sobs. It was a performance so convincing and so frightening that Frank Dobson never dared to question any item of expenditure on the wedding from that time onwards.

Emma went on serenely planning the event according to her own standards of perfection, hiring a harpist to provide background music for the reception, and a band for dancing in the evening, retaining the services of a stills photographer and a video film-maker to record every moment of the day, instructing a florist about the buttonholes and table decorations that would be required, booking her favourite hairdresser to come to her parental home on the morning of the wedding to style her hair, choosing the design and composing the wording of the invitations, drawing up a list of desired presents to be filed with John Lewis for the convenience of donors, and of course ordering her wedding dress from a specialist shop. It was made of white satin and lace, inspired by Kate Middleton's wedding dress, and required several fittings. When Mrs Dobson saw her in the finished garment, she wept tears of pride and joy. Twin cousins of Emma's agreed to be bridesmaids, very happy to be dressed identically (which was not always the case), and the six-year-old son of another relative was to be a page in a Little Lord Fauntleroy suit, holding up the train of the wedding dress as Emma processed down the aisle of the church. She had a low opinion of weddings in registry offices and other secular buildings. Only a church would provide a proper setting for her marriage, and though neither she nor Neville were actively religious, they had both been baptised into the Church of England. Solihull's fine medieval parish church was available, but there was no parking space anywhere near it and the guests would have to drive or be driven after the service to Longstaffe Hall. There was a little old church in the village of Longstaffe which would be perfect, and Emma persuaded its initially hesitant vicar to marry them there on the spurious grounds that she and Neville intended to look for a house in the area in due course. This was the item on her checklist over which Emma had least control, and it was a great satisfaction to her when she placed a tick beside it. Everything was going according to plan.

All this time Neville was content to leave the preparations for the wedding to Emma, and she of course was happy to shoulder the responsibility. He gave his approval to the various decisions she reported to him – rather distractedly, because he was very busy at work, focused on an imminent trip to Dubai, where he had a complex audit to carry out. There was a little contretemps when he resisted her suggestion that he should wear morning dress for the wedding, but she managed to talk him into it. Their first serious disagreement was provoked by her proposal that they should abstain from sex until the honeymoon, which was to be a ten-day holiday in the Maldives.

'What on earth for?' he said, staring.

'Well, I've been thinking,' she said. 'I've been thinking it would make the whole thing more meaningful – and more exciting. I mean, a honeymoon must feel like just another foreign holiday if you've been having sex as usual right up to the wedding day. If we gave it up now, from now till our wedding night—'

'That's nearly three months off!' Neville exclaimed.

'But imagine how much we'd be looking forward to it, as the time approached,' Emma urged. 'Dreaming of it, longing for it. It would be a real honeymoon.'

'What am I supposed to do in the meantime – wank?'

'Don't be disgusting,' Emma said.

'It's all very well for you,' he grumbled. 'But a man needs physical relief, especially after working hard all day – or all week. Weekends wouldn't be the same without sex.'

'Just make an effort to do without for a while, pet, for my sake. You won't regret it.' She gave him a look suggestive of unbridled licence to come if he agreed. There were certain variations of the sexual act which Emma had so far declined to perform when Neville proposed them, and she could see he was intrigued by the implied bargain.

'Well, I'll see,' he said. 'I'll see how it goes.'

Two weeks later, just before Neville was due to go to Dubai, Emma was sent on a weekend course at a hotel in the country near Bristol, convening on Friday and ending on Monday, but on Saturday morning a fire broke out in the kitchen, which was so badly damaged that the course was cancelled and they dispersed at midday. On the way back to Birmingham she tried to phone Neville, but his mobile was switched off. She let herself into the flat and called out, 'Neville! It's me,' but there was no answer. When she entered the living room the first objects that caught her glance were a blouse and brassiere, not her own, on the floor beside the sofa. She stood stock-still and stared at them, hyperventilating.

Neville, wearing a bathrobe, appeared at the door which led to the bedroom and closed it behind him. 'Hallo, Em,' he said, with a sickly attempt at his famous smile. 'What happened to the course?'

'You've got a woman in there,' she said.

He sighed and raised his hands in a gesture of surrender. 'Yes.'

'Get her out.'

'She's dressing.'

'She'll need those, won't she?' Emma nodded contemptuously at the discarded blouse and brassiere.

At this point the door opened again and a young woman with tousled shoulder-length hair entered the room. She wore jeans and had covered her buxom torso with a jacket. 'Hallo,' she said to Emma. 'This is embarrassing, isn't it?'

'Get out of my house,' Emma said.

'Absolutely,' said the woman, as she scooped her clothes from the floor. 'I would feel the same.' Emma had to admit to herself later that the slag showed considerable poise in the circumstances.

'Who is she?' Emma asked when the woman had gone.

'Someone from work.'

'How long has this been going on?'

'It hasn't been going on. This was the first time. We had a bit of a snog at the office Christmas party, but nothing else.

We bumped into each other this morning at Starbucks . . . got talking and moved on to Strada for lunch, and a bottle of wine. She said she'd like to see the flat because she was thinking of getting one in this area herself, so I asked her up. One thing led to another . . .'

'I can't believe you could do such a thing,' Emma said furiously. 'Just ten weeks before we were supposed to get married!'

'But that's just it, Em,' he said. 'If you hadn't concocted that stupid ban on sex before the wedding, this would never have happened.' He registered belatedly the phrasing of her last remark. 'What d'you mean, *"were supposed* to get married"?'

'You don't think I would marry you now, do you?'

'What, just because of a single shag?'

'But in my own flat! In my own bed! How could you?'

'I'm sorry, Em,' he said, and moved towards her with his arms wide.

She shrank back. 'Don't touch me! Go away. Leave me alone. I have to think.'

Neville put on some clothes and slunk out of the flat, and Emma sat down to think. Neville's infidelity was a great shock. He had fallen irrecoverably from grace in her regard, and she would never be able to trust him again. How could she possibly go through with the wedding? But then, she reflected, how could she not? How could she bring herself to tell her parents, her relatives and friends, that the wedding was cancelled, the engagement was broken, and for the most sordid and humiliating of reasons? Her parents would be aghast, her wider family shocked and scandalised, her friends and colleagues variously pitying, excited, amused and in some cases, whom she could name, secretly gleeful when they heard the news. Going to work would be a daily ordeal instead of the pleasure it had always been. Then the arrangements for the wedding were so advanced, due to her own diligence, that it would be fiendishly difficult and hideously expensive to dismantle them. Her father had already paid a substantial non-returnable deposit on the cost of the reception and – it came back to her with a pang – she had laughed aside the idea of insuring against cancellation when the Functions Manager suggested it. The wedding dress could not be cancelled, and must be paid for, but she would never wear it, for one thing was certain: if she abandoned this wedding, she would never have another one like it. If she were to marry someone else at some time in the future, it would have to be a quiet, unostentatious affair that would not revive memories of this nuptial debacle or require another lavish outlay of cash by her father.

Perhaps, Emma thought, she could find it in her heart to forgive Neville.

He returned late in the evening, looking, she was glad to note, suitably chastened, even grim, and sat down facing her. She made a prepared speech about how much he had hurt her but perhaps the experience could be turned into something positive. It was better that something like this should happen before marriage rather than after, because it had brought into the open the issue of fidelity, which was for her absolutely essential. She knew he believed men had different needs and urges from women, but he was wrong. At this point she made a personal confession. 'You remember that alumni reunion at Bath I went to last summer? I met Tom, a fella I used to go out with in my second year, in fact he was the first boy I slept with. He was doing computer science. We were very close, but then I did my year abroad in France and after a while he wrote to say he was seeing someone else. When I came back for my final year he'd graduated and left the uni. Well, at the reunion we caught sight of each other at the drinks reception at the same moment, it was like a scene in a film, you know, across a crowded room, we were transfixed, spent the whole evening together, sat in a corner of the bar, and hardly spoke to anyone else. Tom was still single, getting over a relationship that didn't work out, he said, and I could see he was hoping to get it on with me that night, joking that the beds in the student accommodation we'd been given were much more comfortable than in our day, and as for me, I fancied him rotten, but at the end of the evening I just gave him a kiss and a hug and went to my room. Because of us.'

Neville received this anecdote impassively. Slightly disappointed, Emma wound up her speech: having thought about yesterday's episode very carefully she had decided that if he promised that nothing like it would ever happen again, she would forgive him, and go ahead with the wedding.

Neville took some time to reply. Then he cleared his throat and said, 'Well, I've been thinking too, Em, and I've decided it won't work.'

'What won't work?'

'Our getting married.'

'What do you mean?' A qualm of uncomprehending dismay coursed through her whole body. 'Why did you ask me to marry you, then?'

'I didn't,' he said. 'You told me that we were going to get married, and I agreed. And that's what's wrong with our relationship in a nutshell.'

A long argument followed. Emma tried to frighten him, as she had frightened herself, by listing the consequences of cancelling the wedding, but failed. There would be a fuss, he said, but it would soon be over. 'Of course it doesn't matter so much to you as it does to me,' she said bitterly, 'nor would it cost your family a penny.' 'Better a broken engagement than a broken marriage,' he said sententiously. She changed to a conciliatory tack, admitted that she was over-assertive and promised to be more relaxed and accommodating in future; she recalled good times they had enjoyed together which showed how admirably suited to each other they were; she tried tears. Neville remained unmoved. He slept on the sofa that night, while Emma sought oblivion in the bedroom with temazepam.

The atmosphere in the flat on Sunday morning was frigid. Neville was due to fly to Dubai the next day, and would be away for a week. 'I won't be able to move my stuff out until I get back,' he said. 'Don't say anything about this to your parents, or anybody else, until then,' Emma said. 'I'm not going to change my mind while I'm away, Em,' he said, 'if that's what you're hoping.' 'I'm not,' she said. 'I wouldn't marry you now if you got down on your knees and begged me. But there's going to be a hell of a row and I'm damned if I'm going to face it on my own.' 'Fair enough,' he said, and began packing a suitcase.

Emma in fact had another motive for requesting his silence. As she lay awake in the early morning after the effect of the temazepam had worn off, brooding on the imminent implosion of her perfect wedding, a wild and outrageous idea had occurred to her. So she wasn't going to marry Neville in June – good riddance to him, now she had seen how little he valued her qualities – but suppose she married someone else? Suppose she married Tom?

She hadn't been entirely candid in relating the story of her reunion with Tom. As they shared a bottle of wine in a corner of the bar after dinner, he had told her how wonderful she looked, how often he thought of her and the great times they'd had together as students, what a pity it was that her year abroad had separated them when he was too young and immature to realise that she was exceptional, a girl worth waiting for and keeping faith with. 'There've been other women in my life since then, Emma, but no one like you,' he said. When she told him she was engaged to be married he looked genuinely disconsolate. 'Well, he's a lucky man,' he said with a sigh. As for herself, the meeting revived all the personal charm and intense physical attraction Tom had possessed for her in youth, and the evening ended not with a single kiss and a hug, but a prolonged snog on the bed in his room, to which he invited her for a nightcap from a flask of whisky he had there. She managed to part from him with honour technically intact, but with disordered clothing and emotions, and woke next morning somewhat shocked in retrospect by her own behaviour but relieved that nothing more serious had happened. When they said a restrained public goodbye after breakfast in the refectory he slipped a business card into her hand. 'Thomas Radcliffe, B.Sc., M.Sc., Systems Consultant,' it stated, with a London address and other contact details, and on the reverse side there was a handwritten message: *'Let me know if there's ever anything I can do for you. Tom.'* Well, now there was something he could do for her.

Emma found Tom's card in the wallet where she kept business cards and emailed him to say that her engagement had been broken off, that she was feeling lonely, and would be glad to see him again. He responded immediately: *'When? Where?'* In a rapid exchange of emails it was agreed that he would come to Birmingham the next day and take her to dinner in one of the city's Michelin-starred restaurants. He told her he had booked a room for the night at the Hyatt hotel, but she changed the linen on her bed that morning in case an alternative scenario developed.

They met at the restaurant, and it was soon clear to her that the same thought was in his mind. When he asked her where she lived, and she explained that it was very near and that she could show him the flat after dinner, he wore the expression of someone for whom Christmas had come very early, and scarcely attended to the waiter's conscientious recitation of the ingredients in the exiguous starters he set before them. While they were waiting for the main course to be served, Tom commiserated with Emma on the break-up of her engagement. 'It was a lucky escape,' she said dismissively. 'He wasn't worthy of me. Did you ever think of getting married?' Tom wrinkled his brow. 'Not really. I never met someone I felt I could live with for a lifetime.' 'What about me?' Emma asked boldly. Tom looked startled, laughed, then, seeing that the question was not intended as a joke, adjusted his countenance accordingly. 'That was first love, Emma, for both of us,' he said solemnly. 'We were very young – marriage was out of the question.' 'But it isn't now,' Emma pointed out. 'Er . . . no,' he said. Two waiters appeared at that moment with a pair of plates covered by chromium-plated domes, which were lifted off with synchronised precision under their noses. 'But we're two different people, Emma,' he said, when they had gone. 'We haven't met for years, apart from that reunion last summer. Perhaps we could start seeing each other again, occasionally . . . Who knows what might develop? This concoction looks interesting – how's your fish?' 'The thing is,' she said, 'there really isn't a lot of time, if we're to take advantage of the arrangements that have already been made.' She told him about them in some detail.

Emma had to go to the Ladies between the pre-dessert and the dessert, and when she returned to their table found Tom frowning at his iPhone. He pocketed it as she sat down. 'I'm terribly sorry, Emma,' he said. 'But there's a bit of an emergency in London I've got to attend to.' After he had gobbled his dessert (Emma left hers untouched) he escorted her to the lobby of her apartment building and kissed her chastely on the cheek before hastening off to catch a late train to London. 'Let's keep in touch,' he said. Alone in the lift Emma screamed loudly all the way up to the seventh floor, and pounded the padded walls with her fists. There was a message on her landline from her mother to say that the wedding invitations had been printed and delivered, and would she like to come over some time and help to address the envelopes. And there was an email from Neville saying that he would have to stay on in Dubai for another week, and he thought they should not wait any longer to announce that the wedding was off. Emma took two temazepam and went to bed.

The next day her mother phoned her at work about the invitations. 'If you're too busy to come over, darling, I'll send them out myself.' 'No, don't do that,' Emma said. 'They might have to be changed.' 'Changed?' Mrs Dobson repeated, wonderingly. 'Why?' 'There might be a mistake in the wording,' Emma said. 'I must check them myself.' 'Well, don't leave it any longer, darling,' Mrs Dobson said. 'Time is running out.' 'I know it is,' Emma said. 'I'll come over as soon as I can.' In the background she could hear her father say crossly, 'Tell her it can't wait any longer.'

Her last resort was the internet. She found a website called The Hitching Post where singles could make contact with potential marriage partners without revealing their own identities, and posted an enticing description of herself and a list of the attributes she desired in a husband which concluded, 'Must be available for wedding on the last Saturday in June.' She got a number of replies with surprising speed, some apparently serious, some amused, some obscene. One sent her a photo of his erect penis. A man who described himself as a college lecturer aged thirty-five sounded possible, and as he lived near Birmingham she arranged to meet him in the tea shop of the Museum & Art Gallery. He said he would be wearing a red scarf for identification. She said she would be wearing a silver quilted ski-jacket. In fact she wore a beige raincoat, so that she could observe him covertly before introducing herself. She arrived early for the appointment, but he was already there, with a cup of tea before him, and a soiled red scarf round his neck, reading a newspaper. He was grey-haired, with a straggly beard, and looked as old as her father. As she watched, he picked his nose vigorously, examined the excavated mucus on his fingernail, and put it in his mouth. Emma went hurriedly to the Ladies and was sick.

It was raining when Emma left the Art Gallery. She pulled the hood of her raincoat over her head, thrust her hands into its pockets, and wandered aimlessly along the canal towpaths. Finally, she accepted defeat. She could not persist any longer in denial that the wedding was a lost cause. She began to admit to herself that her recent behaviour had been irrational – irrational and dangerous – driven by a desire not to be married, but to impose her will on a stubbornly resistant reality. What a fool she had been to imagine, when Neville let her down, that she could find another man to replace him in a matter of weeks. She came to a halt, and stared down at the black waters of the canal.

'Excuse me, but are you all right?'

She turned to find a young man in anorak and jeans standing a few yards away. He had his hood up too, but as if conscious that this might seem threatening he pulled it back, revealing a round freckled face and a mop of fair curly hair which had quite the opposite effect.

'I don't want to intrude,' he said. 'But . . .'

'You were afraid I was going to throw myself in?'

'It crossed my mind,' he said. 'You had that look about you.'

'It wouldn't be any use,' she said. 'I can swim. Rather well, actually.'

'Yes, I can believe that,' he said. 'So you're all right?'

'Yes, thank you.'

'OK.' He walked on a few paces, and then turned back. 'D'you feel like a drink, by any chance? There's a nice little pub along here.'

'All right,' Emma said.

'Excellent.' He extended his hand. 'I'm Oscar.'

She shook his hand. 'Emma.'

'So what do you do, Emma?' he asked her, when he brought their drinks from the bar – a vodka and tonic for her and a beer for himself – and sat down opposite her at a small table.

'I work in a bank,' she said. Usually she answered this question by saying 'I'm a banker', because it sounded more important, but she guessed that for Oscar the word would have ugly associations with unscrupulous men earning huge bonuses for gambling recklessly with other people's money and causing the credit crisis. 'What about you?' she asked.

'I'm a conceptual poet,' he said.

'What's conceptual poetry?' she asked.

'It can be anything in words that you present as poetry. You don't have to make it up. You just find it.'

'Where?'

'Anywhere. Weather forecasts, small ads, football results . . . The more ordinary it is, the better. I'm working on a long narrative poem at the moment which is a transcription of the satnav instructions for a journey from Land's End to John o' Groats. It's called *Turn Around When Possible.*'

Emma laughed. The sound surprised her and she realised that she hadn't laughed for a long time. 'You mean you just copy out the directions? That doesn't seem very original.'

'Originality is an ego-trip. Conceptual poetry humbles itself before the miracle of language itself. You don't impose your will on it.'

'That's interesting,' Emma said.

'Of course, with *Turn Around When Possible* I had to choose the journey, and drive the route, so the poem is original in that sense.'

'Can you recite some of it?'

'Sure.' He fixed her gaze with his bright blue eyes, which seemed to her like the eyes of an angel, and intoned in a lilting, melodious voice: '*Cross the roundabout, second exit, then cross the roundabout, third exit . . . bear right, then keep to the left . . . keep to the left . . . in two hundred yards, take the exit and join the motorway . . . exit ahead! . . . in eight hundred yards take the exit . . . take the exit, then turn right . . . turn right . . . . . . turn around when possible.*'

'That's lovely,' Emma said, entranced by the sublime purposelessness of the exercise.

★ ★ ★

Several days later Emma arrived at her parents' house, summoned by an angry message from her father, left on her voicemail. 'What's going on, Emma?' he demanded, as soon as he had closed the front door behind her. 'Neville's parents phoned us this morning. He's sent them an email from Dubai, saying you'd broken off the engagement and the wedding is cancelled. They seemed to think we knew. I didn't know what to say.'

'It's true,' Emma said. Her mother, who came into the front hall in time to hear this, burst into tears. 'Oh Emma!' she wailed. 'The invitations have all gone out! Why?'

'He cheated on me,' Emma said. 'I was prepared to forgive him but he'd changed his mind about getting married.' She gave them a brief account of the episode.

'What a bastard,' Mr Dobson said, softening his tone, and putting a comforting hand on Emma's shoulder. 'I've a good mind to sue him for the cost of cancelling the wedding.'

'There's no need to cancel it,' Emma said. 'All we need to do is have new invitations printed.'

Mr Dobson removed his hand and Mrs Dobson gaped at her. '*What?*' they said simultaneously.

'There's no need to cancel the wedding, because I'm in love with another man who wants to marry me, and he's available on the last Saturday in June,' Emma said.

Her parents exchanged alarmed glances. 'Who is he? What does he do? How long have you known him?' Mr Dobson demanded.

'He's called Oscar and he's a poet and I met him four days ago. On a canal towpath.'

'I told you, Mabel,' Mr Dobson said. 'She's having a nervous breakdown. It's this wedding. It's all been too much for her. She needs help.'

'I don't blame you for thinking that,' Emma said. 'I admit I have been a bit mad lately. But I've never felt saner in my life than I do now.'

'Sane? You call it sane to marry a man you met four days ago? And a *poet*? There's no money in poetry.'

'Oscar has a private income, which I shall manage for him more sensibly than he does now.'

'How much?'

'I don't know exactly.'

'Of course you don't. The man's a confidence trickster, obviously. I know what it is – you've become obsessed with this wedding, and you'd marry anyone, I believe you'd marry the dustman, rather than cancel it. You'll make a laughing stock of us. Well, I'm not going to let you. I'm going to cancel the whole thing. And don't ask me to pay for another wedding one day.'

'All right,' Emma said equably. 'We'll get married quietly in a registry office, without a reception.'

This made Mr Dobson pause for thought, since it suggested that Emma really did love this poet for his own sake. He became even better disposed when he discovered that she had met Oscar's parents, that his father was a High Court judge and his mother a well-known newspaper columnist, and that his private income was an annuity left him by his godmother, a Lady Somebody. By the end of the day Mr Dobson had come round to the idea of having Oscar fill the place of the despicable Neville. Mrs Dobson was pleased for Emma but still apprehensive about the likely reaction of their relatives and friends to the last-minute change of groom. 'Let 'em laugh up their sleeves, if they want to,' said her husband. 'The main thing is that Emma will be happy.'

And she was. The last Saturday in June was breezy and cloudy, but the sun came out and shone on the bridal couple as they emerged from the Longstaffe parish church. Emma looked radiant. Oscar looked angelic. The reception at Longstaffe Hall went off perfectly. The best man, a friend of Oscar's at university, made a speech alluding wittily to the revision of a minor detail in the original invitations, which provoked much laughter. Emma squeezed her husband's hand under the table and smiled serenely. For this reason, if no other, everyone present would always remember her wedding.

# My Last Missis

Near Chelmsford

That's my last missis, hanging on the wall over there, looking as if she was alive. Yeah, she was beautiful, no question. Larry Lockwood took the picture. Cost me an arm and a leg. He was very trendy at the time – his stuff was in *Vogue*, *Harper's*, all the posh magazines. He had an exhibition in the West End, Viv persuaded me to go and see it, said she fancied having her portrait taken by him. When I saw the prices, I said, how about we start with a passport photo? I was only joking, of course. I indulged her. We hadn't been married all that long. Lockwood came down here in his Land Rover with two assistants and a whole pile of equipment – lights, screens and those umbrella things, and set 'em up in the library. Well, I don't do much reading, to tell you the truth – just as well because he stayed a whole week. We have a guest apartment in the annexe next to the pool, so I couldn't very well say no. A week, just to take one fucking photo! Well, of course there was more than one, he took fucking hundreds of them, but he wasn't satisfied, said he was searching for the perfect shot. Yeah, I think he got it in the end – to his own satisfaction, anyway. And Viv's. Go on, have a good look at it. Yeah, an interesting expression. You're not the first one to say that. Or to wonder what it expressed. It wasn't anything to do with me, I can tell you. I wasn't there. I watched Lockwood at work at first, but I got bored fairly soon, and left them to it. She told me it was taken at their last session. Perhaps Lockwood said something specially complimentary to her – that was his style. 'Lovely, darling,' he would say. 'Wonderful, wonderful. Just give me a little more with the eyes.' He called everybody darling, I couldn't object, though I didn't like it. 'Just hold it there for a second, darling, while I change the lens. You have amazing cheekbones, did you know that?' Viv lapped it up. She was always very susceptible to flattery. Didn't matter who it was, a photographer, or her hairdresser, or the guy who checks the chemistry of the pool in the summer. She liked people and they liked her – a bit too obviously for my liking. She encouraged them. She had no taste in people, that's what it came down to. I mean, I'm not a snob. I'm a self-made man. Brought up in a council flat, left school at sixteen with a few GCSEs, and made my money in waste disposal. Started small with a second-hand lorry. Now I've got a fleet of barges going up and down the Thames. When a man's had that sort of success I reckon he's entitled to a bit of respect in his home. When Viv paid her hairdresser – he used to come to the house till I put a stop to it – she would give him a handsome tip and thank him with a smile just the same as when I gave her a diamond necklace for her birthday. If the gardener cut a rose for her when she went round the flower beds she would bring it back indoors with a silly grin on her face, sniffing at it as if it was a line of coke. This began to get on my wick. We had words about it. Mostly her words. I hadn't reckoned on that when I married her. She was little Miss Mouse then, pretty but docile. Couldn't believe her luck: big house, her own car, servants . . . But it went to her head, she started answering me back, cheeking me, till one day I smacked her. That stopped her smiles, I can tell you. It wasn't a hard one, just a slap, but the way she carried on you'd think I'd broken one of her precious cheekbones. Next thing I know she scarpers when I'm away on business, moves in with her parents and sues me for divorce, using all the jewellery I'd given her to pay for a lawyer. Yeah, I was very disappointed in Viv. I'm an old-fashioned guy, I believe the wife should treat her husband as someone special. That's why I contacted your agency. I've heard Oriental wives are very good that way, do what they're told, don't argue, study the husband's needs, you know what I mean? And the photo you sent me of . . . whatser name . . . that's it, Kulap, she looks very nice. I wanted to check out the deal with you in person, and I'm satisfied it's legit, so thanks for coming. When we've agreed a date I'll fly out to Bangkok to meet her, and if it goes well, tie the knot. Oh yeah, Viv got her divorce – and a ridiculous payoff. The divorce law in this country is a joke, except for the poor bugger who has to cough up half his hard-earned money. That's what the judge awarded Viv, half my assets. Would you believe it? Fortunately she died before my appeal came to court, so all it cost me was the lawyers' fees. Car crash. She was on her own, no witnesses, so nobody knows why her Mini went off the road into a ravine. It's a mystery. I felt sorry for her when I heard, in spite of everything. So I keep her picture in here, to remember her by. Wouldn't want anyone to think I bore her a grudge. Shall we go down to the poolside bar and have a drink? You look as if you need one. I've got a nice selection of single malts, if that's your tipple. This way. That's me outside Buckingham Palace when I got my MBE. Now that *did* cost me. The gong, I mean, not the photo.

# Afterword

'The Man Who Wouldn't Get Up' was written in the winter of 1965–66, when I was in very low spirits. I was suffering partly from withdrawal symptoms after a euphoric year in America with my wife and two children, on a Harkness Fellowship, and partly from acute dissatisfaction with the badly built, meanly proportioned and inadequately heated two-bedroomed house we returned to in Birmingham, combined with despair of finding a better one that I could afford. One of the characteristic symptoms of depression, and the closely related state of anxiety, is that at the moment of awakening from sleep one is immediately reminded of the immediate cause or causes of it. One longs, hopelessly, to return to the oblivion of sleep; one puts off as long as possible the moment of rising; and yet even as one clings to the warmth and passiveness of the dozing state one is guiltily aware that sooner or later one will have to get up and face the new day and its responsibilities. (Or so it seemed to me when I wrote the story. In old age I find this predicament has acquired a new and ironic twist: I wake very early, and could easily turn over and go back to sleep because I am retired from regular employment and can do as I please, but I'm wide awake and at the mercy of every negative thought that my brain can muster. So to escape them, I get up.)

It will be obvious how this experience generated a fictional story about a man who *didn't* get up, whose dissatisfaction with his life, and craving for the warm, womb-like comfort of bed, impelled him to defy all the sanctions which ensure that, in the end, we do get up. The story began as a kind of wish-fulfilment fantasy of escape; but as I worked on it, the question of whether the fantasy should be sustained to the very end, or defeated by reality, had to be settled. The man becomes a kind of folk hero, a secular saint, and has delusions of grandeur: *he seemed to see angels and saints peering down at him from a cloudy empyrean, beckoning him to join them . . . with a supreme effort, he wrenched the bedclothes aside and flung them to the floor.* In the story as submitted by my agent to the *Weekend Telegraph* the text continued: *He was aware of cold and darkness. He was in space. 'What do you think you're doing?' said his wife. 'The alarm hasn't gone yet.'* In other words the whole experience described in the preceding pages had been a dream, and he was back where he always was, at the beginning of another depressing day.

I was not entirely happy with this ending, because awakening from a dream is such a narrative cliché. The editor of the magazine wasn't happy about it either, though he liked the story otherwise. Couldn't the man die, he suggested, or simply get bored with lying in bed and get up? The latter suggestion was too banal to consider, but the first one prompted me to write the ending with which it was eventually published. I decided that death should come to the man in the form of the drab physical environment with which he had begun his withdrawal from life, represented by a detail in the original description of the room, *the long jagged crack in the ceiling plaster that ran like a sneer from the electric light fixture to the door*; and I inserted a passage about this crack having been repaired and concealed by redecoration earlier in the story, its reappearance creating an effect of the uncanny appropriate to the revised ending. This ending punishes the central character more severely than the original one, and turns the story into something of a macabre cautionary tale. But perhaps I was teaching myself a lesson by writing it.

The basic premise of the story is similar to that of the late Sue Townsend's novel *The Woman Who Went to Bed For a Year*, published in 2012, and they have some narrative elements in common. Her heroine, like my central character, becomes a popular celebrity as result of her refusal to get up, and there is even a crack in the ceiling above her bed which she invests with symbolic significance. I do not suspect any influence. Such ideas would easily occur to any writer developing the same *donnée,* and it is very unlikely that the nineteen-year-old

Sue Townsend was reading the *Daily Telegraph* in 1966, when my story was first published.

'The Miser' was originally written for radio, and broadcast by the BBC in the 1970s (I cannot remember exactly when). It was based on a personal experience in childhood, a year or two after the end of the War – my friends and I really did find an old man miraculously selling pre-war fireworks out of a hut on a golf course – but the denouement was invented. I chose to tell this story as if it were a fragment from the early life of Timothy Young, the hero of my novel *Out of the Shelter* (1970), though it was written after the novel. Like the first part of that novel, its style imitates the early chapters of James Joyce's *A Portrait of the Artist as a Young Man* and the short stories of childhood in his collection *Dubliners*, where everything is focalised through the consciousness of an immature central character.

'My First Job', first published in 1980, is another story based on the memory of an episode in my own early life – a vacation job I took when I was seventeen, between leaving school and going to university. I made my adult narrator a sociologist, rather than the novelist and literary critic I eventually became, to bring out the social and economic ironies of the narrative, and gave him a family background quite different from my own. The little gold chain that holds up Mr Hoskyns's palsied lip was borrowed from the father of a childhood friend of mine. It was an object of some fascination to me then, and I have never seen such a device worn by anyone else.

'Where the Climate's Sultry' was first published in 1987, but drafted some years before that, and looks back even further in time. As the sexual revolution of the Sixties and Seventies took hold on British society, travel agents began to advertise package holidays on the Mediterranean for the 18–30 age group which promised potential customers unlimited opportunities for sexual promiscuity as well as sun, sand and sangria. Wryly (and perhaps enviously) comparing the visions these advertisements summoned up with memories of holidays abroad when I was a student, before the advent of the Permissive Society, I composed this comic quadrille of sexual frustration among four young Brits raised to fever pitch by their temporary exposure to a holiday under the Mediterranean sun in the 1950s.

'Hotel des Boobs' has a similar theme, but the story, and the writing of it, belong to the 1980s and middle age. In 1985 my wife and I took a short touring holiday in the south of France, staying at a number of pleasant hotels, each with its swimming pool. Most of the female guests sunbathing on the margins of these pools would, as a matter of course, remove or roll down the tops of their swimming costumes. (The practice is not so widespread nowadays.) A heterosexual Englishman of my generation could not be indifferent to this spectacle, though etiquette demanded that one pretended to be quite oblivious to it. Musing on the paradoxical, unspoken code of manners that governs the baring of female breasts in such settings was one source of my story. The other was a curious incident connected with Graham Greene.

I had met Greene on two occasions in England, and corresponded with him occasionally. His fiction had been a powerful influence on my own efforts in this field in youth and early adulthood, and he was kind enough to offer favourable 'quotes' for the jackets of two of my novels. He invited me to visit him at his home in Antibes on the Côte d'Azure when the opportunity arose, and I took up the invitation at the beginning of our holiday. After giving us gin and tonics in his modest flat overlooking the marina, he took us to lunch at a harbourside restaurant. He talked freely and entertainingly about his life and work.

It seemed to me that I ought to write down my recollections of this meeting, and I was doing so the following day, sitting beside a hotel swimming pool somewhere in rural Provence, surrounded by the usual display of bare bosoms, when suddenly without warning a small whirlwind blew through the grounds of the hotel, knocked over chairs, tables and umbrellas, snatched all my manuscript pages high into the air, and carried them away across the countryside. Dismayed at the prospect of losing them, and urged by my wife, I jumped into our rented car with her and pursued the fluttering pages for a kilometre or two, until we saw them settle among trees on a hill which seemed to be a private estate. We followed a winding track which led us to a large ramshackle house where a lady was seated at a table on the veranda – writing. I began to feel that I was in a dream, or a film by Buñuel. It turned out that the house was a kind of retreat for Parisian academics, of whom the lady was one. She was very charming, and amused by our explanation of why we had appeared on the property. She led us to the hillside where we had seen the pages settle, and amazingly we recovered several of them, somewhat soiled but still legible. This curious adventure, combined with my meditations on the subject of topless sunbathing, prompted the story of 'Hotel des Boobs'.

When I returned to England I wrote to thank Greene for his hospitality, but resisted the temptation to mention the incident of the *petit mistral*. I was sure it would have amused him, but I didn't want to admit to writing down my recollections of our conversation, since I had not asked his permission to do so. Probably he wouldn't have minded, but I didn't want to risk undermining a relationship I valued highly.

'Pastoral' was commissioned by BBC Radio in 1992, for a series of stories to be broadcast in the intervals of classical music concerts. A number of writers were shown a list of well-known symphonies and concertos, and invited to write an original short story which had some connection with one of them. Seeing on the list Beethoven's Sixth Symphony, the *Pastoral*, I was reminded of a Nativity play I had written and produced in my youth for the Catholic parish in south-east London to which I belonged, in which the 'Shepherd's Song' was used as incidental music, and wrote this story. A few years later I drew on the same experience (which is factually described in my memoir *Quite a Good Time to Be Born*) for an episode in my novel *Therapy*. Dedicated readers of my work may find some amusement in tracing the resemblances and differences between these two fictional versions of the same event.

The last two stories in this book were written quite recently. 'A Wedding to Remember' is set in the present century, in and around Birmingham, where I have lived since 1960 when I was appointed assistant lecturer at its oldest (and at that time only) university. It has changed a great deal since then, and like other English industrial cities has redeveloped its centre to accommodate service industries, leisure facilities and various hedonistic pursuits, including fine dining (a concept which would have seemed risibly incongruous when I first arrived there). Unlike the previous stories this one contains nothing that is derived from my own experience except the location. The basic idea came from an anecdote told to me by some friends, concerning a family only distantly known to them who lived in another part of England. A daughter of this family was engaged to be married, and a big, expensive wedding was arranged, but after invitations had been issued the engagement was broken off for reasons unknown. Instead of cancelling the wedding, however, the young woman married someone else at the arranged time and place. My friends, who were not present at the occasion, did not know any more details. I regarded it as a kind of challenge to a writer of fiction to imagine how such a marriage might possibly come about, and the result was 'A Wedding to Remember'.

Obviously it was the young woman's story, and obviously she had to be a strong-willed character, determined to bend the world to conform to her own wishes. I called her Emma, suggesting a faint resemblance to Jane Austen's heroine, who is rewarded with her Mr Right only after a humbling lesson in self-knowledge. The sexual mores of her age group and class are different from those portrayed in the earlier stories. Cohabitation is now a lifestyle taken for granted by the younger generation, and accepted more or less reluctantly by their elders, but the longer it goes on in any particular case, the more of an issue the possibility of marriage becomes, especially for the woman, and infidelity is almost as serious a breach of trust in this kind of relationship as it would be if the couple were married. Since weddings nowadays are mostly of people who have been sexual partners for some time, they have lost much of their traditional meaning as a rite of passage – hence, perhaps, the increasing amounts of time and trouble and money that are lavished on them to create a theatrical sense of occasion. (An article in my daily newspaper informs me that 'A best man will no longer suffice for some couples, who order an owl trained to fly down the aisle to deliver their wedding rings.') Emma Dobson, self-appointed producer of her own wedding, is determined that the show in which she has invested so much must go on, even if it requires a last-minute recasting of the groom. She is lucky to get away with it.

'My Last Missis' is the latest of these pieces and was published in the Autumn 2015 issue of *Areté*, a literary magazine with a small, select readership, edited and produced on a shoestring by Craig Raine. It originated with the thought that Robert Browning's poem 'My Last Duchess' was, among other things, a perfect short story, and might provide a model for another one in a modern context that would contrast entertainingly with the original – not as parody, but as *hommage*. The line *'That's my last missis, hanging on the wall'* floated into my head, and I went on from there. The first line of Browning's poem is actually, *'That's my last Duchess painted on the wall'*, indicating that the portrait of the Duchess was a wall-painting or fresco, but I imagined as my modern equivalent a large framed photograph hung on the wall.

'My Last Duchess', which was first published in 1842, is a dramatic monologue, a poetic form of which Browning was a supreme exponent and which he applied to many historical and contemporary subjects. It differs from a simple monologue (such as my story 'Pastoral') in that it gives one side of a conversation between two people, so that the reader must infer the responses and reactions of the interlocutor to the speaker's words. This greatly increases the effort of interpretation required of the reader, and in this case intensifies dramatic tension as the true nature of the situation emerges. Although 'My Last Missis' is a complete story on its own, I hope it will be enhanced by the reader's awareness of its intertextual dimension. 'My Last Duchess' is a well-known and much admired poem, frequently studied in schools, colleges and universities; but inevitably some of my readers will not be familiar with it, and even those who are may not recall it in every detail. For the benefit and convenience of both groups I therefore append the text of Robert Browning's poem. The word 'Ferrara' underneath the title locates the story in his favourite territory, Renaissance Italy. The speaker is thought to be based on Duke Alfonso II d'Este of Ferrara (1533–98), who married the fourteen-year-old daughter of Cosimo I de' Medici, Grand Duke of Tuscany, whose lineage was less distinguished, for the sake of her dowry, and was suspected of poisoning her two years later.

## My Last Duchess
### Ferrara

That's my last Duchess painted on the wall,
Looking as if she were alive. I call
That piece a wonder, now; Frà Pandolf's hands
Worked busily a day, and there she stands.
Will't please you sit and look at her? I said
'Frà Pandolf' by design, for never read

Strangers like you that pictured countenance,
The depth and passion of its earnest glance,
But to myself they turned (since none puts by
The curtain I have drawn for you, but I)
And seemed as they would ask me, if they durst,
How such a glance came there; so, not the first
Are you to turn and ask thus. Sir, 'twas not
Her husband's presence only, called that spot
Of joy into the Duchess' cheek; perhaps
Fra Pandolf chanced to say, 'Her mantle laps
Over my lady's wrist too much,' or 'Paint
Must never hope to reproduce the faint
Half-flush that dies along her throat.' Such stuff
Was courtesy, she thought, and cause enough
For calling up that spot of joy. She had
A heart – how shall I say? – too soon made glad,
Too easily impressed; she liked whate'er
She looked on, and her looks went everywhere.
Sir, 'twas all one! My favour at her breast,
The dropping of the daylight in the West,
The bough of cherries some officious fool
Broke in the orchard for her, the white mule
She rode with round the terrace – all and each
Would draw from her alike the approving speech,
Or blush, at least. She thanked men – good! but thanked
Somehow – I know not how – as if she ranked
My gift of a nine-hundred-years-old name

With anybody's gift. Who'd stoop to blame
This sort of trifling? Even had you skill
In speech – which I have not – to make your will
Quite clear to such an one, and say, 'Just this
Or that in you disgusts me; here you miss,
Or there exceed the mark' – and if she let
Herself be lessoned so, nor plainly set
Her wits to yours, forsooth, and made excuse –
E'en then would be some stooping; and I choose
Never to stoop. Oh, sir, she smiled, no doubt,
Whene'er I passed her; but who passed without
Much the same smile? This grew; I gave commands;
Then all smiles stopped together. There she stands
As if alive. Will't please you rise? We'll meet
The company below, then. I repeat,
The Count your master's known munificence
Is ample warrant that no just pretence
Of mine for dowry will be disallowed;
Though his fair daughter's self, as I avowed
At starting, is my object. Nay, we'll go
Together down, sir. Notice Neptune, though,
Taming a sea-horse, thought a rarity,
Which Claus of Innsbruck cast in bronze for me!

# For the Man Who Wouldn't Get Up – Hommage to David Lodge

by Philippine Hamen

The way that a reader can react to a story he read, and loved, can take different forms: in this case, it is a piece of furniture. *For the Man Who Wouldn't Get Up* is a response addressed to the eponymous short story, and thanks to the enthusiastic initiative of David Lodge, this collaboration between literature and design has resulted in an exhibition at the Ikon Gallery of Birmingham, and in a new edition of the very book in which I encountered the story.

'The Man Who Wouldn't Get Up' tells the story of a man who is tired of life, tired of getting up every morning to live the same day indefinitely, and who one morning simply refuses to get up, after he realises that he 'only loves this: lying in bed'. The hero, or rather anti-hero, eventually executes his plan, which is to stay in bed. He becomes a local but ephemeral celebrity, and when after months, or years, he finally wants to get out from his bed, it is too late: he is now too weak to get up.

The story had such a vivid impact on my imagination, and I could relate so well to the fictional man who wouldn't get up, that it fed me with the desire to create a piece tailor-made for this character, who lies secretly inside each of us, and to overcome the lack in the furniture landscape of a surface from which one can read or work while comfortably lying down, equidistant between a bed, a chair and a desk. *For the Man Who Wouldn't Get Up* is thus a hybrid piece of furniture, of a new type: a lounger cantilevered upon a desk. This 'lounger desk' (it needs a neologism) provides an appropriate ergonomic structure and uses the principle of the 'face hole', featured usually in massage tables, to allow the user to read or work lying face down, enabling him to 'stay in bed' and 'be at the office' simultaneously.

The lounger desk questions the long-held association of verticality with the activity of work, whereas horizontality is mostly associated with idleness, perceived in a very negative way by our capitalist societies which sacralise hard work. In that regard, 'The Man Who Wouldn't Get Up' could be seen as the visionary model of the anti-hero produced by service sector society. The temptation to stay in bed when we have to go to work or to school is universal; a miniature rebellion against the hyper-productive ideal of our system; a regressive drive to remain in a safe, warm, womb-like environment; but spoiled either by the resolution to get up or by guilt about not doing so. The lounger desk would be a solution to this dilemma as it aims to reconcile within a unique space the work sphere and the domestic sphere, the desk and the bed; and could be an artefactual response to French surrealist poet André Breton, who exhorted us to 'overcome the depressing idea of the irreparable divorce between action and dream' (*Les Vases communicants*, 1932).

*For the Man Who Wouldn't Get Up* might be seen as a utopian piece of furniture, but it is a serious ergonomic response to the postural problems that our service sector society, coupled with the domination of the chair/desk, has generated. In a typical Western lifestyle, most of us spend daily, like the hero of this fiction, 'eight hours' drudgery in a poky office', most of these hours spent sitting down, and mostly in a bad posture. Lower back pain, acute and chronic, along with many other disorders, is the natural consequence of bad posture, and one of the main reasons for absence from work.

The human spine is designed specifically to support the standing-up posture of man, not to sit down at 90 degrees. When we sit down on a chair, several things happen: the back and abdominal muscles that support the trunk relax, so in order to compensate for stability and to fight gravity, we soon get into a slouching posture, where lumbar lordosis (concave) flattens or even reverses into kyphosis (convex), but constantly keeping an 'ideal' upright posture to maintain the spinal curves would be very tiring for the back and shoulder muscles. Because, when we sit, most of our body weight rests on our two small sitting bones, we have to keep shifting from one side to the other to relieve pressure, resulting in an asymmetry of the spine. Lastly, when sitting down, our blood flow tends to be compressed by the thighs and to accumulate in the lower part of the legs, making us constantly fidget to avoid swollen legs. As we see, we have become very good at compensating for the shortcomings of the chair, which even the thickest upholstery can barely counterbalance, instead of questioning the validity of the archetype.

The design of the lounger desk is an attempt to solve these shortcomings. Its horizontality allows an even distribution of the body weight, stability is assured simply by gravity, the curvatures of the spine are respected (the angle of the chair, at 142 degrees, is approximately the same as that of the spine), and finally, the elevation of the feet prevents the blood from accumulating there. Just as on a massage table, we can lie prone and symmetrically, and while through the hole we can read a document placed on the 'desk' part, the arms hanging on each side at a comfortable angle, the hands resting, we can turn pages, write or type. If the purpose of sitting is to relax those muscles that are not involved in the task, then the lounger desk performs this function better than the classic chair. Of course, there is no such thing as a perfect chair, or a perfect posture, because we need to keep moving, otherwise we might end up like The Man Who Wouldn't Get Up!

*For the Man Who Wouldn't Get Up* may be the bizarre fruit of a wonderful winter tale, full of poetry and dark humour, and of pragmatic, down-to-earth ergonomic considerations – but beyond that, as the subtitle 'Hommage *to David Lodge*' indicates, it is a tribute to the man behind the story, who had such an important effect on me as both reader and designer.

penguin.co.uk/vintage